Harvey Angell and the Ghost Child

"Did you . . .?" Mr Perkins began.

"Yes," said Henry. "Did you . . .?" He wondered if his own face was as pale as Mr Perkins'.

"I thought I saw . . ." said Mr Perkins. It was as if he might make the ghost child real if he put her into words.

"A girl," said Henry. "You saw . . . I saw . . . a girl."

"A ghost," said Mr Perkins, beginning to shiver. "A ghost girl. And then only bits of her."

"I saw all of her," said Henry. "I think your torch frightened her away."

"Are you thinking what I'm thinking?" asked Mr Perkins after a long silence.

Henry looked at him. Was there, suddenly, in the ghostly stillness of the hidden room, a charge of telepathic energy as though a single thought flashed between them?

"I'm thinking," said Henry, "that we need Harvey Angell."

DIANA HENDRY BOOKS IN RED FOX

Harvey Angell
Harvey Angell and the Ghost Child
The Awesome Bird

Harvey Angell and the Ghost Child

Diana Hendry

RED FOX

For Hamish – with love

A Red Fox Book

Published by Random House Children's Books
20 Vauxhall Bridge Road, London SW1V 2SA

A division of Random House UK Ltd
London Melbourne Sydney Auckland
Johannesburg and agencies throughout the world

5 7 9 10 8 6 4

First published in hardback by Julia MacRae 1997

Red Fox edition 1998

Printed and bound in Great Britain by
Cox & Wyman Ltd, Reading, Berkshire

RANDOM HOUSE UK Limited Reg. No. 954009

Papers used by Random House UK Limited
are natural, recyclable products made from wood grown in
sustainable forests. The manufacturing processes conform to
the environmental regulations of the country of origin.

ISBN 0 09 922052 0

CONTENTS

From ghoulies and ghosties and long-leggety
beasties
And things that go bump in the night,
Good Lord, deliver us!

Anon

CHAPTER 1

Henry was worried about his Aunt Agatha. She was not her old mean and miserable self. It was true she still counted her tea bags at night and no one could say that the portion of potatoes she spooned out at supper time to Henry, Mr Perkins, Miss Muggins and Miss Skivvy was exactly generous, but for all that Aunt Agatha was a changed woman.

Aunt Agatha was happy! Trillingly, smilingly, chillingly happy! A rainy day, awful news, a terrible cold – nothing seemed to dim Aunt Agatha's happiness. It was curiously bothersome, as though Aunt Agatha had lost her weather, had no spring, summer, autumn and winter any more, only one long and constant smiley summer.

It was not that Henry wanted the old Aunt Agatha back – Aunt Agatha of the wintery withers, Aunt Agatha who kept both her piano and her heart tightly locked and whose sorrow had filled 131 Ballantyre Road with a dusty grey gloom; Aunt Agatha as she had been before the arrival of Harvey Angell. No, Henry certainly didn't want *that* Aunt Agatha back.

Harvey Angell had changed not just Aunt Agatha

1

but the whole house. He had changed 131 Ballantyre Road from a House of Sorrow to a House of Happiness.

"Watts and volts, watts and volts, better by far than thunderbolts," Henry often sang to himself when he remembered how for one brief week in the summer Harvey Angell had come to live in the attic. What strange gear he had pulled out of his electrician's tool bag on that first morning! A bundle of screwdrivers with brightly coloured handles – well, they'd been ordinary enough – but after them came what Harvey Angell called his Connecting Kit, his Energy Charger and the magical Centuries Clock.

At first Henry had thought that Harvey Angell was up to no good, sniffing about the house as he did, going off to graveyards and playing his silver flute. It made Henry grin to think how he and Mr Perkins had played detectives, following Harvey Angell through the city streets and ending up at the amazing Waifs and Strays Café.

It was there, over a Supernova burger, that Henry had learnt about Harvey Angell's strange profession of 'Homer'. It was a job, Henry thought, that was something like an electrician's and rather more like a *mag*ician's.

"What I do," Harvey Angell had said, cheerfully tucking in to Earthly Bangers and Mash, "is connect the living and the dead. We're all on the same circuit, you see." (That was the electrics.) "Only people forget that. They switch off, like you switch off an electric light!" Sorrow, Harvey Angell had explained, made people switch off and the Energy – the energy that was a kind of love – was switched off too. What Harvey Angell did, what all Homers did, was connect

2

people up to the Energy Supply. And that was the magic. And that was what he'd done at 131 Ballantyre Road. He'd released Aunt Agatha's sorrow. He'd switched them all on again. He'd connected them to the Energy.

But, Henry thought, was it possible that a little too much Energy had got into the circuit and that Aunt Agatha – and Mr Perkins too, for that matter – had somehow been super-charged?

Henry remembered how Mr Perkins, quiet and sober Mr Perkins, had danced about in the graveyard in his pyjamas, declaring himself divinely sparked and thinking this was a huge joke. A 'spark', Mr Perkins had said, was the slang word for an electrician and now he, Mr Perkins, had been divinely sparked – and he'd gone off to the park to write a soppy love poem about Aunt Agatha. Mr Perkins was deep in unrequited love for Aunt Agatha and Aunt Agatha said this was good for him (as if love was like spinach or vitamin pills) because it sharpened his verse.

And now, in his super-charged state, Mr Perkins had bought himself half a dozen pairs of pyjamas and appeared regularly in the park as a Performance Poet. He'd taken to clicking his fingers between lines and pushing back his few remaining wisps of hair and flinging his arms about. It was all extremely embarrassing to Henry.

And Aunt Agatha, in her extra-happy state, was no better. Aunt Agatha had taken to pushing the piano out into the street every Friday morning and busking there, much to the amusement of the boys at school who wanted to know if Aunt Agatha was planning to go on *Top of the Pops* and if everyone in Henry's house was a nutter – including Henry.

'Henry Oddity' they called him and they had a rhyme they sang. They sang it in the playground. Sometimes, walking home from school, a trio of girls would sing it behind his back,

"Henry Oddity
What a clod is he
A curiosity
Henry Oddity."

Henry hated it. He badly wanted to be just like everyone else. And even more badly he wanted a friend. It wasn't just the goings-on of Aunt Agatha and Mr Perkins that made the others nickname him Henry Oddity and left him feeling lonely, clumsy and cloddish, it was the clothes!

Aunt Agatha bought him jumble-sale clothes. Henry didn't mind the oldness of the clothes – indeed he thought old clothes were much more comfortable than new ones. But Aunt Agatha never took Henry with her when she went Jumbling (as she called it) and as a result nothing fitted properly. Henry had trousers that were too short, too long, too baggy or too tight and jerseys that looked as if they'd been knitted by someone who was colour blind. Henry must have been the only boy in school (apart from Jed Lomax who was another friendless oddity) who didn't have a pair of trainers. When Henry looked at himself in the mirror he didn't notice his warm brown eyes or his friendly smile. He only saw what he thought the others saw – an oddity.

To make matters worse, in her happy state, Aunt Agatha's 'jumbling' grew wilder. Proudly she brought home T-shirts and jerseys in such bright, clashing colours that even Mrs Towers (Henry's class teacher)

said, "My word, Henry, I need sunglasses to look at you this morning!"

The car which Aunt Agatha bought might also have come from a jumble sale. It was a very old, very cheap, rattly Rover. Happiness had not cured Aunt Agatha of her skinflint ways, but it had cured her of greyness. She sprayed the car bright pink and drove it in much the same way as she played the piano – her foot on the loud pedal/accelerator. And for extra cheer, the pink Rover was fitted with a special horn that played the first three notes of Beethoven's Fifth Symphony because, said Aunt Agatha, she wanted to make sure that people knew she was coming. And everyone certainly did!

"Damon Hill rides again," said the boys when now and again Aunt Agatha, wearing teddy-bear ear muffs, took it into her head to collect Henry (whose own ears burnt bright red with embarrassment) from school.

And as if Henry didn't have enough to cope with, even Miss Muggins and Miss Skivvy – who before Harvey Angell's visit had been two shy and timid old dears – were no longer either. Miss Muggins had joined the town's Operatic Society and was currently rehearsing, mostly when Henry was trying to sleep, for HMS *Pinafore*. As for Miss Skivvy, who'd worked in the Post Office for so many years that she'd come to look like a brown paper parcel herself, well, Miss Skivvy had retired and begun doing a sandwich round of the homeless – on a skateboard.

She made excuses about the skateboard, of course. Said her legs were poorly and skateboarding helped her get about. Even though Henry admired Miss Skivvy no end – and sometimes helped her make the sandwiches – it didn't help his image when she whizzed past the school gates at lunch time and the boys called out, "Hey! There goes Skivvy-Saintboard!"

It was just when Henry was wondering if the Energy level in the house might run down just a little and make life more normal, that he came downstairs for breakfast to find Aunt Agatha and Mr Perkins dancing.

Mr Perkins was shaking the tin he used in the park to collect money. And Aunt Agatha was shaking the tin she used when busking on her piano, and together they made a terrific noise. They shook their tins like maracas and Aunt Agatha tossed her skirts and Mr Perkins clicked his fingers high in the air and stamped his feet and Henry had a very hard job making himself heard.

"What's going on?" asked Henry. "Have we won the lottery?"

"No!" cried Aunt Agatha, doing a twirl. "But we've made enough money to go on holiday! We're going to the seaside, Henry!"

Then Henry's heart lurched because for all the years since his parents had died and he'd lived with Aunt Agatha, he'd never been on holiday. And he'd never seen the sea.

Henry's own energy level shot up like the mercury in a thermometer, like a kettle brought to the boil, like a battery re-charged. Super-charged!

"The seaside!" cried Henry and he and Mr Perkins and Aunt Agatha linked arms and danced round the kitchen table.

And in the weeks that followed, super-charged – or sea-charged – was how everyone in 131 Ballantyre

Road stayed. Miss Skivvy bought herself a straw hat, a striped swimming costume and a pair of orange armbands which she wore at supper-time. ("Just to get used to them.") Miss Muggins sang sea-shanties – 'What Shall we Do with the Drunken Sailor' and 'The Big Ship Sails through the Alley Alley O' being her favourites. Mr Perkins recited 'The Seafarer', which Henry thought was a very miserable poem as the Seafarer always seemed very cold. He had icicles in his beard and was missing someone. Mr Perkins also read them a list of names for the sea which he'd found in a book called *The Odyssey*. There was the 'fish-haunted deep' and the 'darkling ripple'; the 'Salty Abyss', 'Ocean's Pouring Stream' and 'The Briny Water' and many more.

Sometimes, Henry lay in the bath practising his back stroke and murmuring 'the boundless sea' and 'the waveworn caves', for the rhythm of these made him feel as if he was in a boat. Afterwards he'd sail a few sponges in the bath water and pretend it was the 'fish-quick sea'. Dreaming of the sea was a kind of escape from loneliness.

Aunt Agatha had a different way of dreaming about the seaside. She spent her evenings counting the money in the busking tins and doing what she called her Holiday Budget. There was no budging Aunt Agatha from her budget. She wrote down everything she could think of that they might possibly spend money on.

"Put down fish and chips," said Mr Perkins.

"And ice cream," said Miss Muggins.

"And candy-floss and rock," said Miss Skivvy. "And perhaps a donkey ride."

Aunt Agatha put down her pencil. "I don't think

it's that kind of seaside," she said. But when they asked her what kind of seaside it was, she wouldn't tell them. It was to be a surprise.

Night after night, Aunt Agatha, Mr Perkins, Miss Muggins and Miss Skivvy talked of seasides they had known. The lights and the big dipper at Blackpool (Miss Muggins); a little Cornish cove (Miss Skivvy); the pier at New Brighton (Mr Perkins); Sea View Guest House on the Gower (Aunt Agatha). Only Henry said nothing. Henry had his own picture of the seaside in his head, a picture that seemed almost too precious to share.

There would be miles and miles of sand, of course. And rocks to clamber about. There would be shining, shimmery, tossing blue waves to dash in and out of. There would be ice-cream three times a day and little boats bobbing in the distance and permanent sunshine. And most importantly your eyes wouldn't be cut short, as they were in the city, by big buildings and huge walls. There'd be 'boundless sea' and 'waveworn caves'. In one of these, Henry imagined, there still might linger an occasional smuggler or pirate. And if there weren't smugglers or pirates there would certainly be an adventure of some sort or another.

And that was one of the few things Henry was right about.

CHAPTER 2

All five of them sat silently in the pink Rover while great waves like lions' paws clawed over the sea wall and the wind rocked and shuddered the car. It was almost midnight.

Henry sat squashed in the back between Miss Muggins and Miss Skivvy. They'd wrapped themselves in the picnic rug.

The journey had taken so long, and they'd eaten so many Homeless sandwiches, that Henry felt a little sick. Sick on tuna sandwiches and sick with disappointment too. What had happened to permanent sunshine? In fact what had happened to summer?

Miles and miles ago Aunt Agatha had put on her teddy-bear ear muffs and kept them on. She'd got fed up with "How far is it now?" (Miss Skivvy) and "I feel a little queasy, dear," (Miss Muggins) and most of all, Mr Perkins' rhymes.

Mr Perkins, it had been revealed, might be very good at reading 'The Seafarer' and Homer's *Odyssey*, but he was no good at all at reading a map. Aunt

Agatha's Happy State became as delicate as a tea-cup perched on a cliff edge.

Instead of road directions, Mr Perkins gave rhymes. By the time they'd gone through,

> "How many miles
> To Carlisle?"

and (when on the wrong road)

> "We should not go,
> My dear, to Stow,"

and

> "Far, far in the North
> Is the bridge 'cross the Forth,"

Aunt Agatha had clamped on her ear muffs and kept them on. Now she took them off in time to hear Mr Perkins say,

> "In Fife, in Fife,
> The wind goes through you
> Like a knife."

"Is that where we are, then?" ventured Henry. "Fife?" Something about the back of Aunt Agatha's head told him that the old Aunt Agatha, Aunt Agatha of the wintery withers, might re-emerge at any moment. Henry wondered why Mr Perkins hadn't chosen to rhyme 'Fife' with 'wife', seeing that he proposed to Aunt Agatha at least once a week. But perhaps this wasn't the moment.

There was a brief silence and then in a determinedly bright voice Aunt Agatha said, "Yes, Henry, that's where we are. In Fife, Scotland. And tomorrow it's going to be a beautiful sunny day and we shall all have a wonderful holiday."

It sounded like an order. "You *will* have a wonderful holiday or else . . .!"

"There, there, dear!" said Mr Perkins, patting Aunt Agatha's hand. "You've had a long drive."

"Do *not* pat and 'there there' me!" snapped Aunt Agatha.

In the back, Henry grinned. He was glad Aunt Agatha had grown happy, but there was something comfortingly normal about her snappiness.

"All we've got to do now is find Tom Troone," said Aunt Agatha.

"Who's Tom Troone?" asked four voices at once.

"He has the key to Sibbald House," said Aunt Agatha, "the house we've rented. He lives at . . . let me see . . ." Aunt Agatha dug about in the pocket of the dashboard and produced a piece of paper. "Ah yes, here it is. Rooftops Cottage, Cove Wynd."

"But will he be expecting us, at this hour?" asked Mr Perkins.

"I said late afternoon," said Aunt Agatha.

"Well," said Mr Perkins, "I suppose you could call this late afternoon. Very late afternoon. Have you directions?"

Aunt Agatha had. Cove Wynd was a narrow alley – far too narrow for a car – running up from the sea road to the High Street.

"A dose of sea air will do us all good," said Aunt Agatha resolutely.

But the wind, when they all climbed out of the Rover, was so fierce that Miss Muggins and Miss Skivvy – with the rug still wrapped round them so that they looked like Siamese twins – had to hold on

11

to each other to stop themselves from being bowled over.

"You'd better wait in the car," commanded Aunt Agatha. "Henry and I will go."

Henry felt nicely important. He grabbed his anorak and dashed after Aunt Agatha who was striding, soldier-like, up the road. The wind ballooned Henry's anorak as he ran. It blew all about him. It blew a great whoosh of excitement inside him. It was as if the wind whipped up his spirits as it whipped up the waves, as it pulled the pins from Aunt Agatha's hair, as it made them both bend and push themselves against it. And all the time the sea rushed and roared up against the sea wall like a creature desperate to escape.

Alarmed clouds scudded nervously across the moon, anxious to get away. The houses of the village were all in darkness as if the people here knew that on a night like this it was best to play dumb. Best to sleep. Far out, Henry could see a light buoy flashing a ghostly green warning. He was on holiday, wasn't he? And if not on holiday, he was on an adventure.

"Wicked, isn't it!" Henry said, catching up with Aunt Agatha. But Aunt Agatha, now short of breath, only grunted and they were both glad when they found Cove Wynd – as winding as its name – and the wind was behind them.

The narrow Wynd with its low cottages seemed snugly defended against both sea and storm. But as they climbed up it, the view of the sea and the cliffs of the coast grew vaster and vaster, until near the top of the Wynd they both stood, gasping for breath and looking down on what, to Henry, looked like an enormous stage where, while everyone slept, some great battle was being played out between sea and cliffs, night and sky.

Tom Troone was not asleep. He was awake and angry. He loomed in the doorway of Rooftops Cottage, the largest, oldest man Henry had ever seen, with as many lines on his face as roads on Mr Perkins' map.

"Call this late afternoon?" Tom Troone growled at them. "More like the middle of the night!"

Nervously they followed him into the cottage.

"I'm afraid we had a bad journey . . ." Aunt Agatha began, trying to stick the pins back into her hair. "We set off in good time but then . . . "

"Makes no odds to me, woman," said Tom Troone. (Henry had never heard Aunt Agatha called 'woman' before.) "No odds at all. Given up on sleep. Day or night. Makes no odds to me. No odds at all. Journeys. Holidays. They're nothing to do with me."

"But you've got the key?" said Aunt Agatha anxiously. "The key to Sibbald House?"

"Oh aye," said Tom Troone, "I've got the key."

Henry lurked just behind Aunt Agatha. There was something alarming about old Tom Troone. He wore thick, baggy black trousers stuck into sea boots that looked as if he never took them off and an old fisherman's jersey that had so taken his shape it was like a second skin. But it wasn't just Tom Troone's size – his long legs and broad shoulders – that was alarming. It was more that he looked as if the sea had battered him as fiercely as it was now battering the cliffs. The sea, Henry thought, had taken chunks out of Tom Troone. It had hollowed his cheeks to gauntness, sharpened his old bones, put a strangely wild and haunted look in his faded blue eyes. And

13

he reminded Henry of someone, only he couldn't think who.

"You've brought the boy then?" Old Tom said suddenly.

"Well, yes," said Aunt Agatha, surprised. "I told you in my letter there'd be four grown-ups and Henry. There's room for that many, isn't there?"

Tom Troone seemed to find this almost funny, for he snorted and said, "Aye, there's room all right. Makes no odds to me how many of you there are."

The old man was fond of his 'odds', Henry thought, and he was just wondering if there were any 'evens' to go with the 'odds', when he suddenly found himself in the middle of the room, under the light, with Tom Troone's hands on his shoulders.

And such hands! Enormous paws, they came out of the sleeves of his jersey like thick tree roots searching for soil and finding Henry instead. For half a minute Tom Troone studied Henry's face and then, just as Aunt Agatha moved to rescue him, the old man said "Hmph!", relaxed his grip and turned away towards the kitchen.

"I'll get you the key," he said.

"Very old!" whispered Aunt Agatha as they waited. "Losing his grip." Henry, who could still feel Tom Troone's grip on his shoulders, felt very doubtful.

While the old man rummaged about in the kitchen, muttering, "Put the thing in a safe place. Makes no odds," Henry had time to look about him. It was a sparse room apart from one wall of old photographs. They were mostly of fishing boats and bearded men in sou'westers smoking pipes, though there was one of a girl carrying a basket of fish on her hip.

There were only two chairs in the room and a small

table covered in a dark blue oilcloth. Beside the fire was an old fishing basket full of driftwood and across the fire, on a brass pole, hung two pairs of thick socks (so the boots *did* come off sometimes!) and a string vest. Henry had a glimpse of the kitchen where a fishing net full of pots and pans was slung across the ceiling.

Then Tom Troone was back, dangling the key from his huge paw. "You can drive to the end of the mid-shore road," he said, "but you'll have to walk from there. Last house on the sea path. And mind the Drench."

"The Drench?" said Aunt Agatha, plucking the key from old Tom's fingers as if she feared he might suddenly snatch it back again.

"High tide," said old Tom, "when the sea tops the wall."

"I see," said Aunt Agatha, passing the key to Henry who pocketed it.

"Any complaints and I don't want to know," said Tom Troone at the door. "You understand? I don't want to know."

"We'll certainly try not to trouble you again, Mr Troone," said Aunt Agatha crisply, pulling Henry outside.

The old man watched them go. Henry thought he was still talking to himself, going on about it making 'no odds' but the wind carried his words away.

Aunt Agatha, now as stormy as the sea, strode down the Wynd as if the conversation with Tom Troone had wound her up like a clockwork toy and set her going on 'fast'. Henry hurried after her.

"What a bad-tempered old man!" said Aunt Agatha, as if she herself had never known a day's ill temper. "Calling me 'woman' like that! Such rudeness!"

Henry couldn't resist. "Makes no odds to me," he said.

"That'll do, Henry!" snapped Aunt Agatha. "The old man is probably round the twist which would explain his rudeness. You, as far as I know, aren't!"

Henry said no more. They were back at the car now. Henry took the key from his pocket and danced it against the windscreen. "We've got it! We've got it!" he sang. A faint 'hurrah' came from Miss Muggins, Miss Skivvy and Mr Perkins. "And we're to mind the Drench!" added Henry. Three pale and alarmed faces peered back at him.

But Aunt Agatha, brisk as the wind itself, flung open the boot and said, "We shall have a splendid sea view. The house is just past those fishermen's cottages," and she pointed to where the beach road ran out and a narrow path ran along the shoreline up towards the cliffs.

The others climbed out of the car. Mr Perkins, as if he was still in the city, put up his black umbrella. At once the wind blew it inside out.

"Use your cagoule!" said Aunt Agatha, thrusting it at him. The cagoule was stiff and crackly but once inside it Mr Perkins perched on an old rope bollard and screwing up his eyes against wind, rain and sea-spray, looked up the path.

"I can see it!" he said. "It's the house at the very end. And you're right, Agatha dear, we shall have splendid views. But we'll have to carry the luggage."

Henry too balanced himself on the bollard and looked towards the house. It was a tall, square house with a steep roof and a great many chimney pots.

Even in the dark it looked plain and severe. Each window had a stone over-hang like the lid of an eye and the house itself seemed to stare gloomily down into the sea. For a moment Henry thought he saw a light in one of the upstairs windows, and then it was gone. Moonlight, Henry thought. Moonlight reflecting off the sea.

Aunt Agatha hitched a knapsack on to Miss Muggins' back.

"But what about this Drench?" asked Miss Skivvy. She had tied a scarf over her straw hat and had pulled her armbands on over her jersey. From the large plastic bag she was carrying Henry could just see the tip of a skateboard.

"The old man's nonsense!" said Aunt Agatha. "Can you manage a bag in your other hand?"

Miss Muggins was the one to get the Drench. Staggering a bit, under the knapsack and with a carrier bag full of books and her knitting, Miss Muggins was watching her feet when the Drench came, a huge wave that flung itself up and over the sea wall and up and over Miss Muggins.

"Ohhh!" she spluttered, "I'm drowning standing up!"

"Run for it!" called Mr Perkins. "Before the next wave comes!"

Sopping and squelching, Miss Muggins paddled – rather than ran – onwards.

"Watch the sea!" ordered Mr Perkins. "It's the seventh wave that's the big one!"

So they watched and counted – all except Miss Skivvy who had grown so nervous she seemed rooted to the spot. Eventually the others had to take her bags and Mr Perkins gave her a piggy-back.

Henry, given a suitcase that seemed full of bricks, struggled along at the end.

"We're nearly there!" called Aunt Agatha.

Henry looked towards the house. It was not a welcoming house. It stood on its own, after the line of cottages, stark stone and mean-windowed. It was too wet and cold to linger outside but inside was not much cheerier. A draughty hall led into a dark pannelled sitting room. There was little furniture and all of it dusty. The sofa and two armchairs looked, thought Henry, as if mould was about to grow on them any minute. The lights, Henry reckoned, must be all of twenty watts and the house looked as if no one had lived in it – yet alone holidayed in it – for years and years and years.

Miss Muggins stood dripping and sobbing on a once-patterned rug. Aunt Agatha hurriedly flung things out of bags until she came on a towel and some dry clothing. Mr Perkins lumped the luggage in a corner and went off in search of wood for a fire. Miss Skivvy, for no reason whatsoever, blew up her armbands and collapsed into one of the mouldy chairs.

It was about two in the morning when at last they were all seated round the fire with mugs of tea (they'd had to wash the mugs first) and some of the chill had gone out of the room and their faces were flushed warm.

"Well," said Mr Perkins, looking severely at Aunt Agatha, "I suppose we all know why you booked *this* house!"

"Cheap!" said Miss Muggins and Miss Skivvy together. "Cheap! Cheap! Cheap!"

Henry giggled.

"Every man has his cross to bear," said Mr Perkins, "and mine is to love a mean woman."

Aunt Agatha glowered at him. "What does the house matter?" she asked defiantly. "We'll be out on the beach all day." The sea, roaring outside and sometimes dashing against the front windows of the house as if it actually wanted to come in, seemed to mock her words.

"Thrifty," said Aunt Agatha. "I think of myself as thrifty, not mean."

But they were all too tired to argue or complain.

The house, they discovered, had three floors. Miss Muggins and Miss Skivvy chose to share a bedroom on the second floor. Aunt Agatha had the other. The top floor contained one twin-bedded long room and a smaller adjoining room. Henry, knowing how Mr Perkins snored, took the smaller one.

He was too tired to explore it but he peered through the small window, murky with sea spray. Below him the sea noise was like an orchestra. He could see the light buoy still flashing its green warning and – yes – the tide was going out and he could see just the beginning of a beach. It was enough to cheer him. Henry drew the thin tatty curtain and climbed into bed. Tomorrow it would all be different. Tomorrow the sun would shine and there'd be ice-cream three times a day. Well, at least once.

He wriggled down into his sleeping bag. But not for long. A rattling window made sleep impossible. Henry got out of bed, stuffed a sock into one corner of the window frame and got back into bed.

The sock muffled the window's rattle, but there were other noises now. Creakings and groanings and moanings. Henry reminded himself that 131 Ballantyre Road had its night noises too, only he was used to them – had, he realised, even grown fond of them. After a night or two here he'd be used to these, he told himself, and pulled the sleeping bag up round his ears.

Briefly he thought again of old Tom Troone. Who was it the old man reminded him of? And just before he fell asleep, Henry remembered. It was the Sea-farer. The Seafarer in the poem Mr Perkins read. How did it go? Something about cold feet (Henry curled up his own) and sitting at the oars 'clenched against clinging sorrow'. That's how old Tom Troone had seemed. 'Clenched against clinging sorrow.'

Henry snuggled deeper into his sleeping bag. He'd seen the beginning of a beach, hadn't he? And tomorrow would almost certainly be sunny.

CHAPTER 3

But it wasn't. It was dull and cold and the sea – as if exhausted by its rage of the night before – had rolled itself back against the sky in a dark grey sulk.

Henry woke up in good spirits. He woke, not to the sound of city traffic, but to the cry of seagulls. 'Where are you? Where are you? Where are you?' they seemed to be calling. Henry got out of bed, set a chair against the window, and rubbing his fist over it in an attempt to clear it, looked out.

The seagulls did indeed seem to be waiting. They were lined up on a long strand of rock like a troupe of tennis players waiting on a railway platform for the train to Wimbledon. And all around them was beach. A perfect bay of beach. A scoop of beach on which a black dog was frolicking. Perhaps, thought Henry, he could make friends with the dog. To dogs, probably all people were oddities. Beyond the bay, beyond where Henry could see, he had the sense of more beach; beach going on forever; a beach that would only stop when the land ran out or time ran out – or both.

Henry pulled on his lime-green (jumble) trousers and two jerseys – the bedroom was chilly – looked at his socks and shoes and decided against them. He wanted bare feet on bare sand.

Everyone else was still asleep. Henry could hear Mr Perkins' gentle, musical snores. Good old Perkins, thought Henry, tiptoeing down the stairs.

Miss Skivvy and Miss Muggins had left their bedroom door open. Henry glimpsed them tucked in their twin beds, in their twin sleeping bags, tidy as sausage rolls. Miss Skivvy's straw hat hung hopefully on her bedpost and her skateboard waited at the foot of her bed as if, thought Henry, Father Christmas had just been and left it there for her. Aunt Agatha's door was closed. She had hung a notice on the doorknob. It was obviously intended for Mr Perkins for it said, 'Do not disturb – even if you have just written a new poem'.

Henry grinned. He knew all too well what Aunt Agatha meant. Mr Perkins, when he had written a new poem, simply couldn't wait to read it to someone – whatever time of day or night it happened to be. A new poem, like an unexpected five pound note, burnt a hole in Mr Perkins' pocket.

Henry went down into the kitchen. In the daylight the house didn't seem quite so unwelcoming. Rather it seemed forlorn. Unloved. Neglected. It reminded Henry of how 131 Ballantyre Road had been before Harvey Angell had come to stay.

Henry found a carton of milk in the ancient fridge and poured himself a mugful. There was a newspaper cutting on the kitchen table and he read it as he drank his milk.

It was a cutting headed 'Holiday Lets'. Obviously

this was how Aunt Agatha had discovered Sibbald House. Indeed there was an asterisk – in Aunt Agatha's scarlet accounts pen – beside the particular advertisement. Henry realised at once why his aunt had been drawn to it.

'VERY CHEAP HOUSE,' the advertisement began, 'five bedrooms, splendid sea views. Child essential. Write Troone, Box number 312.'

Child essential, thought Henry. How odd! Why would a child be essential? Tom Troone hardly seemed the kind of old man who was particularly fond of children. Henry glanced at some of the other advertisements. Quite a few said 'children welcome'. But 'children welcome' was somehow very different from 'child essential', thought Henry. He remembered Tom Troone's grip on his shoulders and the way the old man had stared into his eyes as if asking a silent question. Henry shivered.

But there was a beach out there, waiting for him, and the tennis-playing seagulls still calling, 'Where are you? Where are you?' Henry wiped the moustache of milk from his mouth, crept down the dark hall and out onto the sea path.

He had only to run along it a little way to get down to the beach. The fishermen's cottages all looked a great deal jollier than Sibbald House. Many of them were whitewashed and had bright front doors. Someone had already pegged out a line of washing. The line, strung between two short iron poles, looked as if it was really intended for fishing nets.

Henry jumped down some narrow stone steps and on to the beach. The seagulls, on the platform, rose on tiptoe, shuffled their wings and settled again.

It was, Henry decided, a perfect beach, for it had

everything. (Everything, that is, except a friend to
share it with for the black dog had vanished.) But
there was pale soft sand and arrangements of assorted
shells and pebbles that the sea had grouped together
into shapes as curious as countries on a map. And
there were shelves of rocks with enough smooth, flat
ones to make leaping from one to another easy and
to provide, between them, little clear pools where
green moss floated like miniature forests. And yes,
he was right, beyond the horseshoe of the bay, the
beach stretched on forever. Could it all be explored
in two short weeks, wondered Henry?

The sea was a roll of dark silk, like a long bolster
propped against a bed-head of grey sky. It was too
far out for Henry to paddle but it seemed important
to get his feet wet. You weren't really *at* the seaside
until you'd got your feet wet. Henry sat on a rock
and dabbled his feet in an ice-cold pool.

He was enjoying himself so much that he forgot all
about the strange advertisement until in the distance
he saw a figure coming along the beach. A large,
looming figure. Henry was almost sure it was old
Tom Troone. Whoever it was he was collecting wood.
Henry remembered the basket of driftwood by the
old man's fire. The figure caught sight of Henry and
paused. Henry lifted his hand to wave but the old
man suddenly seemed in a hurry to be off. He gathered up a bundle of wood laid near the steps and
hurried away. Henry watched him disappear then
walked slowly back to Sibbald House.

It was only when he got there and the bleakness of
the house struck yet another shiver in his heart, that
he remembered something else about the advertisement that was strange. Something else apart from

'child essential'. 'Five bedrooms', the advertisement said. Five. So where was the fifth? Henry felt sure that when they were deciding who was to sleep where, he'd seen every room in the house.

The Mystery of the Missing Bedroom, Henry said to himself in his Private Detective voice. It was something else to explore – as well as the beach that went on forever.

CHAPTER 4

ack in Sibbald House everyone seemed as sulky as the sea. They were all short of sleep, tired and crotchety from yesterday's long journey.

"It's wonderful out there!" called Henry, running into the kitchen. "You want to see the beach! There's miles and miles of it!"

"I'm glad *someone's* happy," said Aunt Agatha. She was standing on a chair dusting down a network of cobwebs as long as the lace edging of a petticoat. "At least a century old," said Aunt Agatha to the cobwebs.

Miss Muggins was mopping the floor.

"What are you doing?" asked Henry. "We're meant to be on holiday. It's meant to be two weeks without housework or homework. Without any work at all."

"If we don't clean the kitchen we might not survive two weeks," said Miss Muggins. "Unless you don't mind cobwebs in your cocoa and flies in your chips, Henry."

Henry pulled a face. "Where's Mr Perkins?" he asked.

"Locked in the lavatory writing a stormy sea

poem," said Aunt Agatha, "and I wish he'd hurry up about it."

Just then they heard the lavatory door unlock and Mr Perkins, declaiming his poem, came down the hallway.

> "The waves did toss
> The waves did roar
> And wrecked my hopes
> Upon the shore,"

boomed Mr Perkins, coming into the kitchen with his poem floating on a long piece of lavatory paper.

Aunt Agatha filched the poem from his fingers and replaced it with a long shopping list.

"Not now, Perkins!" said Aunt Agatha. "Not now! Food is what we need. I want you and Henry to go down to the Harbour Stores – I saw it last night – you can probably get everything there."

"Man shall not live by bread alone," intoned Mr Perkins, trying to look grand though all the boast had gone out of him.

"But man might fade away without it," said Miss Skivvy, coming into the kitchen. Miss Skivvy looked strangely oily.

"Whatever have you done to yourself?" asked Miss Muggins, letting the mop drip into a puddle.

"Factor Ten suntan oil," said Miss Skivvy defensively. "They say the sea wind can burn you just as much as the sun. Where are the cornflakes?"

"Henry and Mr Perkins are just going to the Harbour Stores," said Aunt Agatha, hanging a basket on Mr Perkins' arm which was still stretched out in recital mode. "Cornflakes are on the list."

"Philistines!" said Mr Perkins. "Come on, Henry. Let's go."

Henry was glad to be outside again and with someone – even if it was only old Mr Perkins – to tell about the beach and the pools and the great flat rocks you could leap across. And walking along the harbour road they could see all the boats.

The harbour was busy. A large silver chute extending out of the side of the fish market delivered ice into the hold of a trawler moored close by. Most of the boats had tall, brightly painted wheelhouses. To sit in one, thought Henry, would be like sitting on the top front seat of a double decker bus, only you wouldn't be riding the city streets, you'd be riding the waves. On one of the boats an enormous winch was slowly winding up a net that looked large enough to trawl the whole North Sea. Other nets – orange and green – were drying on the quay wall. Fishermen with raw red hands clambered about the boats, sorting out the ropes that swarmed over the decks like fat, ancient snakes. Even within the shelter of the harbour, the wind on the water made the boats seem impatient to be off. Fenders squeaked against the quay wall, mooring warps creaked, waves slapped at the hulls, cabin doors clapped and everywhere there was the sharp, salty smell of fish.

Henry looked at the names of the boats. There was *Our James* and *Minnie Wood*; *Eye of the Wind* and *Constant Hope*; and one old boat in much need of repair. *Troone II*, it was called. Was this the old man's boat, Henry wondered? He must surely be too old to go out fishing now. And had there been a *Troone I*?

He was about to tell Mr Perkins about the odd advertisement saying 'child essential' and the mysterious fifth bedroom, but then he thought better of it. Mr Perkins was of a nervous disposition. It would be unfair to upset him when he was on holiday and anyway, he was quite upset enough by Aunt Agatha putting shopping before poems.

But the boats in the harbour and a shop on the corner announcing 'Fish and Chips' seemed to have cheered Mr Perkins considerably. And the Harbour Stores ('proprietor, Annie MacReadie') cheered him even more.

As Aunt Agatha had rightly guessed, the Harbour Stores sold everything. Not only food and news-papers, but wellingtons and cagoules, potted plants and gro-bags. And what Mr Perkins had spotted was a shelf of notebooks and pads, pens and pencils, envelopes and erasers.

Some people are hooked on chocolate. Some can't eat a single biscuit without finishing the packet. Mr Perkins was hooked on notebooks. Big ones, little ones, ones with lines, ones without, feint and narrow feint, white paper, yellow paper, blue paper – Mr Perkins loved them all. He collected notebooks the way other people collect stamps or beer mats or fossils.

In a flash Henry found him cooing over a small green plastic notebook with a fat band of elastic over the cover.

"Just the notebook for pocket poems," said Mr Perkins, twanging the band.

"You've brought about six with you," objected Henry, who had seen them stacked by Mr Perkins' bed. "Come on. We've got a long list and Miss Skivvy's wanting her cornflakes."

Reluctantly Mr Perkins was drawn from notebooks

to cornflakes, baked beans, tea, coffee, eggs, cheese, potatoes, onions, carrots and so on and on until the basket was full and too heavy for Henry.

Annie MacReadie watched them from her stool by the till, occasionally directing them when there was something they couldn't find.

"There's a load you've got," she said, putting down her knitting. She was a tall, strong-boned woman with her hair in a long dark plait. Under her blue overall, Henry could see the top of a bright purple jersey. Her knitting looked like another.

"We're on holiday," Henry explained. "And we've only just arrived."

"Cupboard's as bare as old Mother Hubbard's," said Mr Perkins.

"I knew you were strangers," said Mrs MacReadie, beginning her quick ditting of the cash register. "You'll be renting one of the cottages perhaps?"

"We're staying at Sibbald House," said Mr Perkins, unloading the basket.

Mrs MacReadie's finger, poised over the till, stopped in mid-air and she sat down on her stool.

"Sibbald House!" she repeated. "You're staying at Sibbald House?"

"Yes," said Mr Perkins cheerfully (for without Henry seeing, he'd smuggled the green notebook into the basket). "It's a bit ramshackle and dusty, but wonderful views."

Mrs MacReadie had recovered herself enough to carry on totting up their bill but her face, Henry noticed, which a moment ago had been open and friendly, now seemed as shut as a village shop on Sunday.

"Must be years and years," Henry heard her say,

shaking her head. "Good sea views all right . . . among other things."

What other things, Henry wanted to ask, but Annie MacReadie was now hurrying through their goods and piling them back into the basket as if she couldn't wait to get rid of them. Mr Perkins managed to slip the notebook into his pocket while Henry packed potatoes, carrots and onions into a carrier bag.

"Did you hear what she said?" Henry asked when they were outside. "About Sibbald House having a good view . . . '*among other things*'?"

"Just making conversation," said Mr Perkins, nursing the notebook in his pocket. "Come on, Henry. I could eat three breakfasts now and then we'll all go and explore this beach of yours."

Henry hurried after him, lugging the heavy bag of veg.

"But what d'you think she *meant*?" he persisted. "And why did she suddenly go all shut-up like that?"

"Probably wanted to get on with her knitting," Mr Perkins called over his shoulder. "Like I want to get on with breakfast. Come *on*, Henry!"

So Henry came on. But slowly. There was something scary about Sibbald House, he thought, and something very sad.

"More like a haunted house than a holiday house, isn't it?" laughed Mr Perkins as they arrived.

Henry didn't laugh back. He was thinking about the light in the window he'd seen, or imagined, on the first night. About the noises he'd heard. The moaning and groaning. And about when he'd get a chance to search for the fifth bedroom.

CHAPTER 5

The chance came that afternoon. After an extra-large breakfast they had spent the morning exploring the beach. It was far too chilly for them to lie on it and sunbathe. Instead they walked.

"I hope I'm going to *wear* my swimming costume," said Miss Skivvy sadly, putting on a woolly jacket.

"Of course you will," said Aunt Agatha. "The weather's going to change any day now." (Aunt Agatha spoke as if she was in personal charge of it.) "We'll have a good brisk walk this morning. Get some sea air in our lungs. Do us all a power of good."

So a good brisk walk was what they had. All along the beach and up the cliff path. The tide had turned and above it white gannets, like a teacher's hasty chalk marks, dashed on the grey sky, dived into the sea at a speed of at least sixty miles an hour.

Henry and Miss Muggins collected shells and pebbles until their pockets were heavy with them. Henry liked the small translucent pieces of sea glass best. Blue, green, white – they shimmered as if the sea had been caught inside them, as if they were small chunks of sea.

Chapter 5

By the afternoon – in spite of Aunt Agatha's weather predictions – the rain was back.

"Torrential," said Mr Perkins, rolling the word around his tongue. "Torrential," he repeated happily.

"Monopoly," said Aunt Agatha. "We'll light the fire and play Monopoly."

But by the time Henry had bought his first hotel for Vine Street, all the old ones had nodded off to sleep. For a moment Henry looked at them in exasperation. Someone his own age, a friend, would never fall asleep at such an exciting moment in the game. He took the 'Chance' card from Miss Muggins' hand and put it back in the box. Clearly Miss Muggins was not going to 'Advance to Trafalgar Square' (or anywhere else) *that* afternoon. But the sleeping elders gave Henry the chance he needed to look for the fifth bedroom.

Where to start? Downstairs there was just the kitchen, sitting room and a small cloakroom off the hall. Surely a fifth bedroom wouldn't be downstairs? All the same, Henry poked about in there, pressing walls in case there was some kind of secret door like you saw in films. There was nothing.

Upstairs then. Henry had just finished examining Aunt Agatha's room when he thought again of the light in the window. Had the light been from the fifth bedroom? If he looked carefully at all the windows of the house and tried to remember – perhaps this would tell him.

He crept downstairs again. Soft snores and snuffles came from the sitting room. Fortunately Mr Perkins had left his umbrella in the hall. Leaving the front door ajar, Henry went outside with it. He stood as far back as he could on the narrow path and looked up at Sibbald House. Counting.

On the first floor: one-two windows (Aunt Agatha's room), three (the landing), four-five (Miss Muggins' and Miss Skivvy's room). Henry looked up to the top floor. One-two (Mr Perkins'), three (the tall landing window that went up both floors), four-five (his own room) – SIX!

Henry nearly dropped the umbrella in astonishment. There it was! A small curtained sash window, just beyond his own room. He lowered the umbrella and dashed inside. It was difficult not to belt up the stairs at full speed, but he didn't want to wake anyone. He took off his wet shoes and ran lightly up the two flights to his own room.

And then it was obvious, blindingly obvious. The built-in cupboard where he'd thrown his jumble clothes in a jumble – this was the only possible way into the fifth bedroom. Why on earth hadn't he thought of it before? Tossing everything out of the cupboard like a burrowing mole, Henry crawled inside it. There *had* to be a way through. There *had* to be a door!

But there wasn't. The back of the cupboard looked just like an ordinary wall. It was only when Henry rapped on it with his knuckles that he realised it was hollow. So there *was* something behind it! For the first time that holiday, Henry actually felt hot. Using his fingers he worked carefully all round the edges of the back of the cupboard. A hidden spring or catch might open it up, he thought. But nothing happened.

It was only when, hopelessly, he let his hands slide down the wood that he felt it move. Of course! It was simple! It was a sliding door. It slid neatly upwards like a hatch, like the kind of garage door that slides up and inside itself. Obviously no one *had* slid it upwards for ages and ages, because it kept getting jammed and Henry had to push first one side and then the other. When it was half open he could wait no longer. He wriggled through.

It was a small room and the dust made him cough. It's a ghost room, was Henry's first thought, for everything in it was covered in white sheets. Or once-white sheets. Sheets that had now turned a pale yellowy brown as though slightly burnt by an iron.

The curtains Henry had noticed from the front of the house were almost white too, but when he looked closely he could see they had once been a blue check. They were so thin that when he tried to open them they fell into tatters.

The room was much narrower than his own but it ran the full side-length of the house so that part of it backed on to Henry's room and part on to Mr Perkins' room. The narrowness of the room allowed for only the one small window at the front. Gingerly Henry began to remove some of the dust sheets.

The room contained a single bed, a small chest of drawers, a dressing table and a wicker chair with most of the wicker rotted away. Henry knelt down and began opening the drawers of the chest. What did he hope to find, he asked himself? This was just an unwanted room, an extra room, an unnecessary room closed off because no one needed it.

And yet . . . and yet . . . there was a strange feeling in the room that made the hairs on the back of his neck prickle. It was as if someone was watching him.

Don't be silly, Henry told himself. The last word seemed to run up and down the room like a shiver up the spine, an echo in the dusty silence. 'Silly . . . silly . . . silly.' It wasn't an unkindly echo. More a laughing kind. But scary. Very scary.

Hastily Henry pulled open the other drawers of the chest. They were all empty apart from a couple of shells. Henry tossed them in his hand for a moment and then put them back.

It was time to get out of here and think. Think what it was all about. He dragged the sheet back over the chest. There was still the dressing table. It was an old-fashioned sort with a swinging oval mirror and a candlestick holder on either side. The dust sheet covered one of them.

Henry pulled it off. A scarlet ribbon hung from the hidden candlestick. Henry lifted it off and ran it through his fingers. It was a broad silky ribbon such as a young girl might wear. He rubbed the dust off it with his finger. It shone now as it must once have shone in the hair of whatever girl it was who'd worn it. The girl who'd slept in this room perhaps. The girl who'd left the shells in the drawer.

On impulse Henry rolled the ribbon in a round, put it in his pocket and crawled out through the sliding door into his own room. It was hard work pulling the door down again, but he was determined to do it. There was no way he'd sleep that night unless that door was firmly closed.

When it was back in place Henry closed the cupboard door too. There was a key in this one. Telling himself he was being ridiculous, Henry locked it, removed the key and hid it in his knapsack.

There! Now nobody could get in. Or out!

CHAPTER 6

Henry found the rest of the day difficult to get through. He could think of nothing else but the hidden fifth bedroom. Part of him itched to talk to someone about it. If only Harvey Angell were here! Aunt Agatha, he knew, would scoff. Miss Muggins and Miss Skivvy would be scared. Mr Perkins was the only possibility.

But Henry hesitated. The room and the scarlet ribbon felt like his secret – and a rather misty secret. How could he say what he feared, that the room was haunted, when the only actual *fact* was the room itself? All the rest could easily be put down to imagination.

Henry fingered the silk ribbon in his pocket and remembered the dusty echo – 'silly . . . silly . . . silly'. It would be silly to tell anyone – yet. He would look again in the room. Perhaps there was something he'd missed, something that would tell him about the girl who'd dreamt and played and slept in there, something that might explain why the room was now shut up.

By early evening the rain had stopped. Miss Skivvy

was out on her skateboard. ("I must have regular practice," she said.) Henry went to watch her. She was very skilled. She could glide gracefully. She could swoop round a corner. With a skier's twist of her feet she could spin to a stop. At a pavement edge, she could make the skateboard leap and come down again without falling off it. Henry perched on a bollard and applauded.

From here he could see the window of the hidden bedroom. Was there a draught making the shreds of curtains shiver? He half expected to see a face at the window.

Supper was a welcome distraction. By a unanimous decision it was to be fish and chips and Henry and Mr Perkins – given detailed instructions about who wanted salt and vinegar and who didn't – were sent to fetch it.

At the door of the fish and chip shop they came face to face with Tom Troone. Tom Troone with a parcel of chips under his arm and in a great hurry. He was still wearing his dark baggy trousers and sea boots, but this time with a matching waistcoat over a thick flannel shirt.

"Watch where you're going, will you!" he cried as Henry trod on his toes.

"Mr Troone!" exclaimed Henry.

"You again, is it?" said the old man and once more he gripped Henry by the shoulders and peered into his eyes. Henry could see the parcel of chips being squeezed tighter and tighter. Again the old man's faded blue eyes stared questioningly into Henry's brown ones. But whatever the old man's silent question was he obviously found no answer for with a kind of frustrated snort he released Henry and hurried out of the shop. "I'm not to be troubled, d'you hear?" he called. "Not to be troubled!"

Henry and Mr Perkins, their mouths fallen open, gazed after him.

"Who on earth – " began Mr Perkins.

"Old Mr Troone," said Henry miserably. "He owns Sibbald House – well, I think he owns it. Either that or he just looks after the key."

"An oddball," said Mr Perkins. "A decided oddball."

For the first time Henry felt a flash of sympathy for old Tom Troone. An oddball. An oddity. Maybe he and Tom Troone had more in common than either knew.

"Perhaps I could write a poem called 'Song by an Old Fisherman' like Blake's 'Song by an Old Shepherd'," said Mr Perkins and there and then, in the middle of the fish and chip shop, Mr Perkins recited,

> "Blow, boisterous wind, stern winter frown,
> Innocence is a winter's gown.
> So clad we'll abide life's pelting storm,
> That makes our limbs quake, if our hearts be
>   warm."

But Henry didn't want to listen to Blake (Mr Perkins' favourite poet) and certainly not in the fish and chip shop. Tom Troone, Henry thought to himself, was a strange and angry old man and nothing like an innocent Old Shepherd. And if you happened to be staying in a house you thought was haunted then there was plenty to make your limbs quake and little to keep your heart warm.

At least the fish and chips – when they ate them

sitting round the kitchen table – warmed Henry's heart. There was lemonade too. Something called *Irn Bru*.

"Good for the muscles, Henry," said Aunt Agatha, pouring him a glassful.

"Is it good for quaking limbs?" asked Henry.

Aunt Agatha looked worried. "Are you feeling all right, Henry?" she asked. "You haven't got a chill, have you?"

Well, thought Henry, he certainly did have a 'chill' but it was not quite the kind of chill Aunt Agatha meant.

"I'm fine," he answered. "But I thought I might sleep on the sofa tonight."

"On that mouldy old thing!" cried Miss Muggins. "It's probably full of fleas."

(Fleas, thought Henry, might be better than ghosts.)

"The window in my room rattles so much it keeps me awake," he said.

"It's a very calm night," said Aunt Agatha. "I don't think it'll bother you tonight."

"And just in case, I'll put a wedge in it," said Mr Perkins.

So Henry, with distinctly quaking limbs *and* a 'chill', made his way upstairs. Halfway, he called down to Aunt Agatha.

"Does Tom Troone own this house?" he asked. "Or does he just look after the key?"

Aunt Agatha sounded surprised. "I don't really know," she said. "He put the advertisement in the paper, so I suppose it's his house. I think it was probably his old family home and now he's the only Troone left and it's too big for him."

"And in too bad a state to sell," added Mr Perkins.

On reluctant legs, Henry climbed the last flight of stairs. Once in his own room he unlocked the cupboard and looked inside to make sure the hatch was still closed. Then he closed and locked the cupboard door again and dropped the key in the bottom of his knapsack. Not that a locked door was much comfort, he thought as he wriggled down into his sleeping bag, for surely ghosts were quite capable of walking through locked doors.

He put the scarlet ribbon under his pillow and lay there, straining his ears for the smallest sound. But Aunt Agatha was right. It was a very calm night. A more silent night than Henry, used to the traffic and the city hum of Ballantyre Road, had ever known. And dark too, for of course there were no street lamps.

The darkness and the silence seemed to melt into each other. But the warmth and snugness of the sleeping bag made Henry feel braver. Tomorrow he would find an opportunity to look round the hidden room again. And then there was another question, a question he hadn't liked to ask himself. What if he went round to Tom Troone's cottage in Cove Wynd – risking the old man's anger – and asked him, straight out, about the hidden room? It was like considering a visit to the headmaster – such an altogether nasty idea that Henry promptly fell asleep to avoid thinking about it any further.

It must have been three or four hours later when he was woken by the noises. They were different from the moanings and groanings of the first night at

Sibbald House. But then this time Henry knew where the noises were coming from.

They began as if someone was moving about in a clumsy, stumbling kind of way. Then there was the sound of drawers being opened and shut impatiently as if the person (Person? Ghost?) was searching for something and getting very cross at not finding it. And then there was loud sobbing.

Henry sat bolt upright in bed. Did he dare? Oh did he dare go and see who was in there? And then he nearly passed out with fright for suddenly his bedroom door creaked open. Henry almost collapsed with relief when he saw it was Mr Perkins.

Mr Perkins in his dear, familiar striped pyjamas. Mr Perkins with his few wisps of hair standing on end and with a torch in one hand. Mr Perkins looking rather shaky. There was more scrabbling and sobbing from next door.

"Henry!" whispered Mr Perkins. "D'you hear that? I'd like to think it was a very loud mouse. But mice don't sob, do they?"

Henry scrambled out of bed. "There's a room," he whispered back. "A room next to this one!" And with a trembling finger he pointed to the cupboard.

"A cup of tea!" said Mr Perkins, giving the cupboard an alarmed look. "That's what we need. A cup of tea."

Hurriedly, over tea in the kitchen, Henry told Mr Perkins everything. About the light in the window. About the advertisement saying 'child essential'. About finding the sliding hatch. About hearing the ghostly echo – 'silly . . . silly . . . silly'.

When he'd finished, Mr Perkins thumped his tea

mug on the table and stood up looking slightly like a mountaineer resolved to attempt Kilimanjaro.

"Well," said Mr Perkins, pulling the cord of his pyjama trousers tight. "There's nothing else for it, Henry. We've got to go and look."

The sobbing had stopped when they tiptoed back to Henry's room. Nervously Henry unlocked the cupboard and pushed up the hatch. It stuck a few inches from the floor and refused to go up any further.

"You first," whispered Mr Perkins, switching on his torch. "You might have to pull me through."

"As long as you follow me . . ." said Henry and then taking a deep breath as if he was about to dive under water, he crawled into the hidden room.

From behind him, the beam from Mr Perkins' torch danced nervously about the room showing up a faded wallpaper of pink and yellow roses.

Henry was just in time to see her. The girl. She was kneeling at the chest. All the drawers had been pulled out. When she saw Henry she leapt to her feet. In the torchlight Henry saw a girl of about his own age, but smaller and with dark curling hair. She wore a blue pinafore over her dress and she stretched out her hands to Henry almost, he thought, as if she was expecting him.

And then, as Mr Perkins heaved and squeezed himself under the hatch, the light from the torch fell directly on the girl's face. The beam seemed to shine right through her. Henry saw her mouth widen into an 'O' of astonishment and slowly, very slowly – and as Henry reached out his own hands and touched only air – she began to disappear.

All Mr Perkins saw when he was finally inside the

room and on his feet was her vanishing hand, a curl of dark hair, the tip of her nose, a toe.

In a state of shock, Henry and Mr Perkins both sat on the bed. Mr Perkins rubbed his eyes and smoothed down his wisps.

"Did you . . .?" he began.

"Yes," said Henry. "Did you . . .?" He wondered if his own face was as pale as Mr Perkins'.

"I thought I saw . . ." said Mr Perkins. It was as if he might make the ghost child real if he put her into words.

"A girl," said Henry. "You saw . . . I saw . . . a girl."

"A ghost," said Mr Perkins, beginning to shiver. "A ghost girl. And then only bits of her."

"I saw all of her," said Henry. "I think your torch frightened her away."

"I think I'm rather glad," said Mr Perkins.

Without saying anything they found themselves holding hands.

"Are you thinking what I'm thinking?" asked Mr Perkins after a long silence.

Henry looked at him. Was there, suddenly, in the ghostly stillness of the hidden room, a charge of telepathic energy as though a single thought flashed between them? The room felt like a glass set vibrating by someone singing a very high note. A tingle shivered through him like wind through dry leaves.

"I'm thinking," said Henry, as carefully as if his voice might break the glass, "that we need Harvey Angell."

"Snap!" said Mr Perkins.

CHAPTER 7

The next morning Henry woke to the sun streaming through his curtains and the sound of Miss Muggins singing, 'O I Do Like to be Beside the Seaside'.

For a moment Henry lay there listening to Miss Muggins. For backing, she had a chorus of seagulls. Summer! It was summer-at-the-seaside at last, thought Henry. The sunshine almost banished away the ghost girl. Surely no ghost could survive such a sunny day? Had he been dreaming last night? Had he and Mr Perkins really seen her?

One look at Mr Perkins' pale morning face told him they had.

Down in the kitchen Aunt Agatha was playing an imaginary piano on the table while Miss Muggins sang. Miss Skivvy was making a swiss roll of her towel and swimming costume. In the hall Henry saw that there was a picnic basket, a beach ball, a rug and two folding deck-chairs all set ready.

Aunt Agatha stopped playing her imaginary piano when Henry and Mr Perkins came in.

"Goodness me," she said, "you two look as if you've seen a ghost!"

Henry and Mr Perkins tried to laugh but Henry's laugh came out as a kind of squeak and Mr Perkins' laugh sounded more like a groan.

Aunt Agatha raised her eyebrows. "I suppose you've noticed the sunshine, have you?" she asked. "Twenty-three in the shade. So hurry up and eat your breakfast. We can spend the day on the beach."

Mr Perkins coughed a few times to get up his courage. "Actually, Henry and I thought we'd go for a walk this morning," he said.

"A walk?" said Miss Skivvy. "No swimming? No sunbathing?"

"I need to consult Henry about a poem," said Mr Perkins. (Well, he was thinking, a letter to Harvey Angell could be called a kind of poem.)

"You can do that on the beach," said Aunt Agatha, fetching her sun-hat.

"I need to try out the rhythm," said Mr Perkins desperately. "I can only do it walking. Like Wordsworth. He walked and talked his poems."

"Well, I hope it's not a long poem," said Aunt Agatha.

"Not very long," promised Mr Perkins. "We'll bring you some ice cream later on. And I'll pay for it," he added, for there was a look on Aunt Agatha's face as if she was trying to add up in her head five ice-cream cornets at sixty pence a cornet.

Aunt Agatha smiled. "Right then. We'll see you later. With ice cream," she said.

When the others had gone off to the beach, Henry got out the letter to Harvey Angell which he'd spent ages writing the night before. He spread it out on the kitchen table and began reading it aloud to Mr Perkins. They had agreed that Harvey Angell was much more likely to respond to a letter from Henry than from Mr Perkins even though, as Mr Perkins was quick to point out, his own letter would have been much more poetical.

Dear Harvey Angell, (Henry began.)

I don't know if the postman delivers letters to the Waifs and Strays Café. I very much hope so.

You see we've all come – I mean everyone from 131 Ballantyre Road – has come to Fife (that's in Scotland and I hope it won't be too far for you) for a holiday. This is because Aunt Agatha is much happier now and she's been busking on the piano and Mr Perkins has been speaking poems in the park, so we've collected enough money.

The trouble is, the house we're staying at – Sibbald House – is haunted. There's a ghost child here. A girl. Both Mr Perkins and I have seen her, though not for long because she vanished when Mr Perkins shone his torch in her eyes.

I am very worried (and a bit scared) and we don't know what to do about her because she seems unhappy. We heard her sobbing in the night.

Please, PLEASE, could you come and help us? I know you are very busy with your Homing work, but we really need you.

Your everlasting friend,

Henry

PS If you come by the sea path, mind the Drench.

"I suppose you have to put that in about the torch, do you?" asked Mr Perkins.

"He has to know the facts," said Henry.

"Well anyway, it's reciting, not speaking," said Mr Perkins a little sulkily. "I don't *speak* my poems, I *recite* them. That's a more musical way of putting it."

"Oh all right," said Henry, rather crossly changing 'speaking' to 'reciting'. "What does it matter? What *does* matter is will this letter reach Harvey Angell? The Waifs and Strays Café is a strange kind of café. You can't always find it unless you're with Harvey Angell or some of his Energy has rubbed off on you."

"Umm," said Mr Perkins. "You've got a point there. I tell you what, I'll write a magic charm on the back of the envelope. That should help."

"What? Something like SWALK – Sealed With a Loving Kiss?" giggled Henry.

Mr Perkins regarded Henry with his most high-brow, snooty look.

"Of course not," he said. "Something like . . ." and there was a long pause while Mr Perkins closed his eyes and massaged his temples.

"Right! I've got one!" he said at last. "Here we go!

"I wash my hands in this thy dish
Oh man in the moon, do grant my wish."

"What's that got to do with anything!" cried Henry, almost hopping with exasperation.

48

"Not a lot," admitted Mr Perkins. "I think it's a charm to cure warts, but it's the only one I know."

"Well, I suppose it will have to do," said Henry.

So Mr Perkins wrote the charm in very small writing on the back of the envelope.

"But what if Harvey Angell doesn't get the letter?" Henry persisted. "Or gets the letter but doesn't come?"

Mr Perkins gave a big sigh. "We'll have to think again," he said. "But there's still Tom Troone. We'll go and see him when we've posted the letter. Perhaps he knows something about the ghost child."

Mr Perkins made a visit to Tom Troone sound quite easy. Perhaps, thought Henry, Mr Perkins was used to angry old men. Sometimes people shouted at him when he was reciting his poems in the park. Mr Perkins didn't seem to mind. ("At least my poem made them feel *something*," he said.) Either that or it was simply that Mr Perkins hadn't known Tom Troone's grip on his shoulders or stood under the old man's fierce, questioning gaze. At any rate, Henry felt glad that he wouldn't have to face the old man alone.

But Tom Troone wasn't to be found. After they'd walked to the Post Office and dropped the letter in the box (with Mr Perkins whispering "Good luck, letter!" down the mouth of the box), they walked up Cove Wynd to Tom Troone's cottage.

They knocked on the door long and loud, thinking perhaps that the old man was asleep, but there was no reply and the curtains, upstairs and down, were drawn.

Mr Perkins tried the house next door but all he got, in reply to his question on the whereabouts of

Tom Troone, was a door opening a crack, an eye and a nose peering out and a voice saying, "Not today, thank you!"

"Well," said Mr Perkins, "let's try Annie Mac-Readie at the Harbour Stores. I should think she knows everyone and everything."

But Annie MacReadie wasn't in the mood for questions that morning. The harbour was quiet with a few boats rocking gently in their moorings and no sign of any of them putting to sea. Annie MacReadie was sitting on a stool outside the Stores, intent on her purple knitting. Despite the sunshine the look on her face was gloomy as a funeral.

"I suppose what you see is a quaint little fishing village?" she said, looking up at them.

"Well yes," said Mr Perkins, taken aback. "It's very pretty and peaceful here . . ."

"And what I see," said Annie MacReadie, jabbing her needles in the purple wool, "is a dying village. Soon it will be tourists we're fishing for, not herring. In the old days you wouldn't have been able to walk along the quay for the men unloading the herring and the girls packing the baskets and barrels and the harbour crowded with boats. No, it wasn't peaceful then. It was alive."

"What's happened to all the fish?" asked Henry, suddenly picturing the sea – like the biscuit tin often seemed at home – empty.

"Progress, they call it," answered Annie Mac-Readie bitterly. "Progress meaning that they learnt such clever ways of catching the fish that soon there weren't any left to catch. And now, though there's some fish, it's rules, rules, rules. Who's allowed what and where and how many. And what *that* means is that more and more fishermen are unable to make a living." And Annie MacReadie clapped her knitting needles together, stood up and went inside the Store. "Now, what can I get you?" she asked, as if on no account either of them were to say how sorry they were about the fish and the dying village.

Henry wondered if sadness for the village explained Tom Troone's ill temper. Perhaps it had nothing to do with Sibbald House. Perhaps it was useless to think the old man could help them.

Mr Perkins cleared his throat nervously. "I *am* sorry about the fish and the fishermen," he said.

Annie MacReadie managed a small smile, reached over the counter and patted Mr Perkins' hand.

"Not your problem, dearie," she said. "You just have a good holiday."

"Thank you," said Mr Perkins. "It was about our holiday, that we've come to see you, in fact. But – er, I will have a tin of cockaleekie soup, please."

Annie MacReadie put the tin on the counter and waited. "You see," continued Mr Perkins, "we're trying to find Tom Troone – he rented us the house, you know. We've been round to his cottage but it looks all closed up. There's just a little something we need to talk to him about."

Mr Perkins spoke as lightly as if the 'little something' was a broken window or a tap in need of a washer. Not a ghost child. But as soon as he spoke Tom Troone's name, Annie MacReadie turned away to the shelves behind her and began busily re-arranging the already neatly arranged tins of soup, beans and rice pudding.

"At certain times of the year," she said, keeping her back to them, "old Tom goes walking."

"Just walking?" asked Henry.

"Just walking," said Annie. "Maybe for days," she added.

"But he will come back?" said Henry.

"Oh aye, he'll be back. When he's walked it out of his system," said Annie. And with that she disappeared into the back of the shop and they had no chance to ask *what* it was, exactly, that old Tom Troone had to walk out of his system.

Mr Perkins put the money for the soup on the counter and called out "Thank you!" but there was no answer from Annie MacReadie.

Outside it was nearly mid-day and hotter than ever.

"Now what?" asked Henry miserably.

"All things considered," said Mr Perkins, "I think it's ice cream and fingers crossed."

"Fingers crossed?"

"For Harvey Angell," said Mr Perkins.

CHAPTER 8

It stayed hot and sunny. Perfect holiday weather.
But neither Henry nor Mr Perkins could relax and
enjoy it. They were jumpy and fidgety. Henry swam
and collected more sea glass. Miss Muggins had lent
him a pair of binoculars and he pretended to be
looking at birds. But really he couldn't stop staring
up the harbour road, hoping, hoping for a sight, a
sound – a *sniff* of Harvey Angell.

In the evening Mr Perkins spent hours gazing
mournfully out of the window.

Aunt Agatha got very fed up with both of them.

"A holiday," said Aunt Agatha, "is about having a
Good Time. It's about Being Happy. And neither of
you are doing it properly."

"Perhaps holidays take practice," suggested Mr
Perkins.

"And perhaps birds need flying lessons," snapped
Aunt Agatha. "Here. You'd better write your post-
cards." She slapped a bundle of cards in front of
them. "Write 'Having a wonderful time'," she
instructed. "That's what you say on holiday post-
cards. Even if you're not."

53

"Yes dear," said Mr Perkins.

"And from now on you *will* have a wonderful time," said Aunt Agatha. "Is that understood?"

"Yes dear," said Mr Perkins again.

"Henry?"

"I *am* having a wonder-full time," said Henry, feeling sorry for Aunt Agatha. "In a funny kind of way," he added under his breath.

They posted the cards in the same box they'd posted their letter to Harvey Angell.

"I don't think he's coming," Henry whispered to Mr Perkins.

"Don't give up hope yet," Mr Perkins whispered back.

They sneaked another visit to Cove Wynd but there was still no sign of Tom Troone.

"Whatever it is in his system, it takes a lot of walking out," said Mr Perkins.

Without Aunt Agatha noticing, Henry had moved and taken the extra bed in Mr Perkins' room. He was prepared to put up with Mr Perkins' snores if only because it was slightly better being scared together than scared alone. But for two nights now there had been no sound from the hidden room. No moaning. No groaning. No sobbing and searching. All the same, both Henry and Mr Perkins slept badly and each night Henry double-checked that the cupboard door was locked. For good measure he propped a chair under the door handle.

By the sixth day of the holiday Aunt Agatha had grown freckles and they were all beginning to look pinky-brown. All except for Miss Muggins, who said she liked to enjoy the sunshine from a shady spot.

Chapter 8

That afternoon she'd found a small cave and sat in its cool entrance reading.

Miss Skivvy, wearing her orange armbands, floated peacefully in the sea, flapping her hands and feet occasionally. Aunt Agatha and Mr Perkins – the latter with a hankie over his face – had fallen asleep in the deckchairs.

Henry wandered down the beach and, finding a wet stretch of sand, wrote his name on it with his finger. Then, rather wistfully, he used a stick and in large careful letters wrote

HARVEY ANGELL

Maybe, he thought, writing someone's name in the sand could work like a kind of magic charm. Certainly he didn't have much hope of Mr Perkins' wart-curing charm. He had just drawn a long squiggly line under HARVEY ANGELL when he heard a roaring noise.

It began as a low hum – much like the city's night-time hum – and grew louder and louder. Henry scanned the sea for motor-boats, but the only boats were far out and utterly silent. In any case, the roaring seemed to come from the sky. It got so loud Henry had to put his hands over his ears.

Aunt Agatha and Mr Perkins were now wide awake, standing up, shading their eyes and staring up at the sky. Miss Muggins had dropped her book and was hiding inside the cave. Miss Skivvy, in a panic, doggy-paddled to shore.

Suddenly there was a terrific wind above their heads. It sent Aunt Agatha's sun-hat bowling down the beach and made Mr Perkins' wisps stand on end.

Then Henry saw it! The helicopter circling above their heads like a huge silver dragonfly with a jewelled tail. Was it . . .? Could it be . . .?

Henry grabbed the towel Miss Skivvy had just wrapped round herself and waved it wildly in the air as the helicopter, its propeller whirling and whirling, sank slowly on to the sand, slithered a little on its ski-like feet, settled and stopped. The helicopter door slid open and a man jumped out, removing a bright yellow helmet.

He was a small, neat man with soft fair hair the colour of thatch, a rather long nose and eyes that might have been green and might have been blue and might have been grey. All you could truly say about them was that they were changeable. He wore denim dungarees, patched at the knees, and carried a canvas tool bag.

The man ducked under the propeller's wings and with a lilting, easy walk came up the beach towards them. His smile was as sunny as the day.

"You called me," said Harvey Angell.

CHAPTER 9

Henry and Mr Perkins had a lot of explaining to do. Aunt Agatha's new freckles almost faded out of existence when she heard of the hidden room and the ghost child. Miss Skivvy grew goose pimples.

"Why on earth didn't you tell us?" Aunt Agatha demanded.

"We didn't want to spoil the holiday," said Mr Perkins.

"Or scare you," said Henry.

"Hmph!" said Aunt Agatha, as if she was totally unscareable.

But as usual, it was impossible for Aunt Agatha to be cross when Harvey Angell was around. It was his smile that did it, Henry thought. How could he have forgotten that magical five hundred kilowatt beam that had enchanted them all in 131 Ballantyre Road? The smile that had lightened the gloom, unwithered Aunt Agatha and connected them all to the Energy. The Energy that was love. Now here they were again, on the beach this time, and sitting round Harvey Angell as if he was the camp-fire at which they warmed their hearts.

Harvey Angell listened carefully as Henry told of the moanings and groanings he'd heard on their first night in Sibbald House and the oddness of the advertisement listing five bedrooms and saying 'Child essential'.

"I never really thought of that," said Aunt Agatha.

Then Henry told how he'd found the hatch into the hidden room, the strange feeling he'd had in there and the echo – 'silly . . . silly . . . silly . . .' laughing at him. (He didn't tell them about the scarlet ribbon. He still felt that was his private secret.)

Mr Perkins chipped in and told how he and Henry had been woken by sobbing in the middle of the night, how they'd gone into the room and seen the girl and how she'd vanished in such a strange way – not all at once, but bit by bit.

"Like the Cheshire Cat in *Alice in Wonderland*," said Miss Muggins, edging closer to Miss Skivvy, "only the Cheshire Cat left his grin behind. Did the ghost child leave her grin behind?"

"No," said Mr Perkins, "the last I saw of her was the tip of her nose and – "

"Does this *matter*?" asked Aunt Agatha impatiently.

"Actually, it does," said Harvey Angell. "It tells us that this is clearly an inexperienced ghost."

"*Are* there inexperienced ghosts?" asked Miss Muggins, but Aunt Agatha gestured her to be quiet. "Not now, Muggins!" she said. "Let's hear the whole story."

So Henry told again of Tom Troone's strange behaviour when they'd called at his cottage for the key and of the unspoken question in the old man's eyes. He told of how Annie MacReadie had suddenly closed up when they'd told her they were staying at

Sibbald House and how she'd hurried away into the back of the Stores when they'd asked her about Tom Troone.

"And now we can't find him because he's gone off walking," said Mr Perkins. "Walking it out of his system."

"Walking *what* out of his system?" asked Miss Muggins.

"That's just what we don't know," said Henry.

"A guilty secret," said Miss Skivvy, who read a great many crime stories. "It has to be a guilty secret."

"Sorrow misshapes us all," said Harvey Angell, standing up and dusting the sand off his dungarees. "Well, time to look at this hidden room, I think. I must say I hadn't expected a seaside holiday."

"But how – " began Henry, and then stopped. How did you get our letter, he'd been going to ask. But Harvey Angell had turned on the full beam and somehow dazzled the question away.

Back at Sibbald House, Mr Perkins led the way up to Henry's room. Henry carried Harvey Angell's tool bag. He knew exactly what was in it so he carried it very carefully. The bag contained Harvey Angell's Connecting Kit – the Centuries Clock that told the time not in hours but in centuries, the Energy Charger and the silver flute. Henry set the tool bag on the bed as tenderly as if there was a newborn baby inside it. Harvey Angell opened the bag up, took out the silver flute and tucked it in the front pocket of his dungarees.

"That's all I need for now," he said.

Henry moved the chair from in front of the cupboard, dug the key out of his knapsack, unlocked the door and then, crawling inside, pushed up the hatch. One by one they crawled after him through the cupboard and into the ghost child's room.

Everything was back in place again. It was as if someone, the ghost child herself perhaps, had been back and tidied up. The dust sheets lay neatly over the bed, the chest and dressing table. Even the drawers in the chest had been put back. In the sunshine – or was it in the presence of Harvey Angell? – the room didn't seem scary any more. Once upon a time, Henry found himself thinking, someone had been happy in here.

They all stayed very quiet as Harvey Angell stood in the middle of the room, eyes closed, hands on his hips, taking deep sniffing breaths. Despite the hush, Henry grinned to himself. Sniffing was Harvey Angell's Thing. Henry remembered how suspicious – how sniff-picious – he'd been when Harvey Angell had begun sniffing about the kitchen and attic of Ballantyre Road. He'd wondered if Harvey Angell was a thief or a kidnapper. But then he'd learnt. Learnt that Harvey Angell was sniffing out the essence of the presiding spirit of the house.

"Same old story," Harvey Angell said now, between sniffs. "Shut off the past and you shut off the Energy – the love that comes through from past to present . . ."

"And on into the future . . ." whispered Miss Muggins.

"Ssshhh!" everyone said.

The past had certainly been shut off in here, thought Henry. Shut off, blocked off, walled off behind a cupboard.

"There are some silences," said Harvey Angell,

"that need to be disturbed." And he took the flute from his pocket and began to play.

Harvey Angell played 'My Bonnie Lies Over the Ocean'. The tune brought tears to Miss Muggins' eyes but the next minute she, like the others, was holding her nose. Mr Perkins had buried his nose in his handkerchief. For as Harvey Angell played an awful smell filled the small room. A strong, salty, pungent stink!

"Uggh!" said Miss Skivvy. "Fish!"

"To be more precise," said Harvey Angell, slipping the flute back in his pocket, "herrings. It's just as I thought."

But for that day *what* he thought remained as secret as whatever it was Tom Troone was walking out of his system.

"Now," said Harvey Angell, "everyone out and I'll tell you my plan of action. And crawl out backwards if you please. Ghosts are easily offended."

CHAPTER 10

"It's like this," said Harvey Angell over supper (it was fresh prawns from the fish market with big fat tomatoes and crunchy radishes), "a ghost is someone who's stuck on the circuit. Someone who can't go backwards or forwards."

"Could someone please explain this circuit to me?" asked Aunt Agatha, spooning a big dollop of mayonnaise over her prawns.

"I can! I can!" cried Henry, sticking his hand up as if he was at school. "It's like the electricity circuit in a house," he began, "that connects up all the lights and the fridge and the cooker and the TV and – "

"All right, I've got that," said Aunt Agatha. "Get on with it, Henry."

"Well, the sort of circuit Harvey Angell deals with is between the living and the dead. I suppose you could call it the love circuit . . ." (Henry blushed.) "Anyway, we're all on it, you see. And to keep the Energy going you've got to stay connected. Switched on! Have I got it right?" he asked, turning to Harvey Angell.

"Absolutely," said Harvey Angell. "You see there

are broken connections everywhere on the circuit. That's what keeps us Homers busy. Something unforgiven. A grief that lasts too long. An old sorrow that prevents new joy. Any or all of these break the connections; stop happiness, stop love, stop Energy, getting through."

They all sat in silence for a while, each thinking of the different sorrows they had known.

A sorrow, thought Mr Perkins, was often like a hard stone in your heart and you had to work on it – like the sea worked on the cliffs – to wear it away. And if you didn't wear it away it wore you away.

"And here in Sibbald House . . .?" he asked. "You said a ghost was someone who was stuck on the circuit."

"Yes," said Harvey Angell. "Stuck. Waiting."

"But for what?" cried Aunt Agatha.

"You mean for *who*?" said Mr Perkins darkly.

Miss Muggins, who had been chewing thoughtfully on a peanut butter and mayonnaise sandwich, her favourite after-supper treat, suddenly interrupted.

"You said our ghost was an inexperienced ghost," she said to Harvey Angell. "What did you mean?"

('Our ghost', thought Henry. It made her sound like one of the family. Yet another oddity!)

"I meant," said Harvey Angell, "that it takes practice being a ghost . . ."

"And until we came she didn't have anyone to haunt!" said Mr Perkins triumphantly. "She was like a poet without readers or listeners. A ghost with no one to haunt because no one's lived here for years and years and years."

"As far as we know," put in Miss Skivvy.

"A ghost doesn't haunt just for the sake of

haunting," said Harvey Angell. "Sometimes a ghost has something important to say. A message of some sort. More often, something to give. He or she is looking for an heir."

"An heir?" said Henry, astonished. "I thought you only needed an heir when you were very old and had pots of money you wanted to leave to somebody."

"Or a stately home," said Miss Muggins.

"Or a library," said Mr Perkins wistfully.

"Or a wonderful grand piano," said Aunt Agatha. Harvey Angell beamed round the table.

"The point is," said Miss Skivvy (who at that moment couldn't think of anything she'd like to be left, apart from youth itself), "what we have here is a ghost *child*. She won't have libraries and pianos to give. I don't see that a child needs an heir."

"That's where you're wrong," said Harvey Angell. "We all have something we need to pass on – something for another person, another generation, to inherit."

"You mean like a talent?" said Mr Perkins. "I believe my great great great grandfather was something of a wordsmith. Perhaps I inherited my poetic genius from him."

"Only it's worn a little thin," said Aunt Agatha. "A bit like your hair." Mr Perkins stroked his wisps and looked hurt.

"It's hard to explain," said Harvey Angell. "Of course an heir might inherit money or a house – a library even. Or it could be a talent. It could be a particular smile. Or a way with dogs. Or a very curious thought that another person – the heir – will carry on and pass on. Eventually that thought might grow into a huge scientific discovery. Whatever it is, big or small, it's precious and shouldn't be lost. None of us know, while we're alive, what our gift to the world will be. But all of us have something to give, something we need to pass on."

"The girl – the ghost child – she was searching for something," said Henry. "She was searching in all the drawers."

"But for what?" asked Aunt Agatha.

"That's what we need to find out," said Harvey Angell. "Whether it's a message or a gift, whatever it is, once she's passed it on, the circuit will be clear again and the past and the present re-connected."

"Like when you get cut off on the telephone and then an operator re-connects you," said Miss Skivvy.

"Much the same," said Harvey Angell with a grin. "Now what I suggest is that tonight we keep a vigil."

"A vigil?" queried Miss Muggins.

"A watch," said Harvey Angell. "Like they do on ships during the night. We'll all take a different watch. My guess is that she's sure to appear to one of us."

"I think I'd rather she didn't appear to me," said Miss Skivvy.

"And I don't think she took to me," said Mr Perkins.

"It wasn't you, it was the torch light," said Henry.

Harvey Angell found a pen and a piece of paper and began working out the hours of the watch.

"If you took an hour each, starting at nine o'clock, that should cover us until two o'clock. I'll do the rest of the night."

Everyone looked rather relieved at this.

"Miss Skivvy can go first," said Harvey Angell. "It'll still be quite light then. And I'd like Henry to do the late watch – from one to two o'clock."

"Henry needs his sleep," Aunt Agatha protested.

"I know," said Harvey Angell. "But I think Henry's the most likely one she'll appear to and that's the favourite hour of ghosts."

They all looked at Henry. Mr Perkins squeezed his hand under the table.

Henry swallowed hard. "Well," he said at last, "I've always wanted to stay up really late. I suppose this is my chance!"

"Good fellow!" said Harvey Angell and he gave Henry such a full-beam five hundred kilowatt smile that it felt like an electric shock of courage running right through him.

CHAPTER 11

H arvey Angell gave them their instructions. 'Good Manners For Ghosts,' he called it.

"Ghosts," said Harvey Angell, "are easily offended and easily scared."

"*Ghosts* are easily scared!" said Miss Muggins.

"So the first thing to remember," Harvey Angell continued, "is that it is *you* who is the visitor, not the ghost. Try not to look shocked or alarmed. Don't speak until you're spoken to and above all don't attempt to do anything silly like shaking hands. Ghosts are greatly embarrassed when anyone tries to touch them."

"You make it sound like an audience with the Queen," said Miss Skivvy.

"It's a great privilege to meet a ghost," said Harvey Angell.

"Like it is to meet a poem," said Mr Perkins thoughtfully. "You have to be very tactful when a poem visits."

"Exactly!" said Harvey Angell. "A ghost, like a poem, is a given grace."

"That's all very well," said Miss Skivvy impatiently,

"but what about that awful smell of herrings? I shall need a peg on my nose."

"I don't think we'll be troubled by that again," said Harvey Angell. "I think the herring smell was what you might call a whiff of the past, not the essence of the presiding spirit. It's my guess that the top of this house was once used as a net loft. It's the sort of house a fisherman would own. A skipper perhaps, because it's much larger than the cottages. The skipper would be the one who made the most money. He'd own the boat and pay the crew. In the days when they used sailing boats – before steam, before diesel – the top of the house was often used to clean and dry the herring nets."

Mr Perkins listened thoughtfully. "Well, if that was a whiff of the past," he said, "are you suggesting that there are lots of ghosts in Sibbald House?" (He looked over his shoulder as if expecting to find one standing behind him.)

Harvey Angell laughed. "No," he said. "There's never more than one ghost to a house. But the past is always present. In the air, you might say."

Miss Muggins was still worrying about the night's vigil. "Couldn't we possibly keep watch in pairs?" she pleaded.

"'Fraid not," said Harvey Angell. "Ghosts like one-to-one conversations. But if it makes you feel better, you can each have a minder."

And so it was arranged that while Miss Skivvy took first watch in the hidden room, Mr Perkins would wait next door in Henry's room and when it was Mr Perkins' turn, Aunt Agatha would wait next door. That way at least they would know that rescue was at hand – should rescue be needed.

Aunt Agatha insisted that Henry should try to get some sleep before the Late Watch.

"But I won't sleep a wink!" protested Henry.

"Well, you can rest," said Aunt Agatha firmly.

"We don't want to take you home a shadow of your former self," said Mr Perkins.

"That is not funny, Perkins!" said Aunt Agatha. "Come on, Henry, I'll tuck you up in my bed."

"I shall play my flute," said Harvey Angell, seating himself at the bottom of the stairs. "Music sometimes eases a ghost's passage, helps to make the connections. Music belongs to our time and all time."

Miss Skivvy and Mr Perkins went upstairs together.

"What time does it get dark?" asked Miss Skivvy nervously.

"Not for a while yet," said Harvey Angell and he gave her the Beam.

Snuggled down in Aunt Agatha's bed, Henry listened to Harvey Angell's flute. It was a jolly sort of tune, he thought, and it reminded him of the sea shanties that Miss Muggins sometimes sang. Yet mixed in with the happiness of the tune was a kind of ache of *un*happiness so that Henry found himself thinking of Tom Troone again and of the Seafarer 'clenched against clinging sorrow'.

What a very strange holiday this was! How would he feel, he wondered, if the ghost girl appeared not to him, but to one of the others? He tried to tell himself that he wouldn't mind. After all, he'd been scared enough that first time with Mr Perkins hadn't he? But something inside him *did* mind.

He wasn't sure how it had happened, but somehow he'd come to think of the ghost child as his friend. They were two of a kind. Oddities. Lonely oddities.

And although of course a real, live friend would be much better than a ghostly one, Henry felt comforted by his feeling that the ghost child needed him, needed him the way a friend would need him . . . if he had one.

He was far too tense to sleep. He lay on his back with his arms behind his head and listened to the song of the flute and the sound of the sea. It was not a stormy night but the tide was up. Henry could hear the waves going 'husha-husha-husha' against the sea wall – as if, he thought, they were smoothing things over, saying all would be well.

What had happened to the girl, he wondered? She could only have been about his age when she died. A whole life unlived. Not that Harvey Angell would see it that way, Henry thought. Harvey Angell would say she was 'on the circuit'. All the same, thought Henry, her ghost, her spirit, had lingered here – perhaps for years and years and years – waiting. Waiting to pass something on. A gift. A message. And in the pit of his stomach – in his very bones – Henry felt that the ghost child had something important to tell him. Something that was only for him.

For no apparent reason it came into his head how, at every end-of-year assembly, the headmaster urged the school's leavers to 'do something with your lives'. The phrase had wafted over Henry's head as something that had nothing to do with him. It was odd how often you could hear something and it didn't seem to mean anything at all. Then suddenly it did, as if the moment was now right, as if you'd been deaf before but could now hear. He repeated the phrase out loud – 'do something with your life'. Surely just living it was enough, wasn't it?

But then, in the moment before he fell asleep, it was as if he was standing outside his life, looking at it, and it was like a film speeded up. Was it possible that you could be haunted by the future as much as by the past?

Henry was asleep before he could answer the question. If there was an answer. But his dream was of the past. In his dream he was walking along the harbour. But it was a far busier harbour than now. It was a harbour much more like the one Annie Mac-Readie had described and all mixed up with the photographs he'd seen on the wall of Tom Troone's sitting room.

Henry dreamt of a harbour crowded with herring drifters and fishermen in sou'westers. In Henry's dream Annie MacReadie turned into a fishwife, standing on the quay, still with her purple knitting but knee-deep in herrings! The boats in Henry's dream were an extraordinary mixture of steam boats with tall hooting funnels and ghostly sailing boats with huge brown and white sails. There were lots of girls too. Girls waiting, like Annie MacReadie, for the boats to come in. They carried baskets on their hips and one of them – a girl with a scarlet ribbon in her dark, curling hair – turned to smile at Henry. Then somehow he was up in the loft of Sibbald House, caught, like a fish, in a huge tangled net and struggling to get free.

"Henry! Henry!" It was Mr Perkins with a mug of tea. "Henry, wake up. It's your watch," he said.

"It feels like the middle of the night!" said Henry,

sitting up and shaking away the dream and the net, the net of time.

"It is!" said Mr Perkins. "It's quarter to one in the morning!"

"Has anyone seen her?" asked Henry anxiously, getting out of bed and pulling on his trousers. (A rather loud tartan that Aunt Agatha had clearly felt appropriate for a visit to Scotland.) Henry felt in his pocket. Yes, the scarlet ribbon was still there. Somehow he thought he might need it.

"Not exactly seen her," said Mr Perkins. "Your Aunt Agatha swears she smelt herrings again and Miss Skivvy says she saw a shadow and Miss Muggins says she heard someone saying, 'Knit me a gansey, there's a dear.' "

"What's a gansey?" asked Henry.

"A fisherman's jersey," said Mr Perkins, who'd learnt this from doing crossword puzzles.

"And what about you?" asked Henry. "Did you see her?"

"I thought someone tweaked my nose," admitted Mr Perkins, turning pink.

"And what does Harvey Angell say?" asked Henry.

"He says," said Harvey Angell appearing at the bedroom door, "that everyone's imagination is working overtime and what we need now is quiet, concentrated attention."

"What is now proved was only once imagined," announced Mr Perkins in his special poet's voice.

"Blake!" said Henry and Harvey Angell.

Mr Perkins looked pleased.

"Nothing *has* been proved yet," said Harvey Angell. "Come on, Henry. It's your turn. You've got Miss Muggins as your minder."

CHAPTER 12

For good luck Henry fingered the scarlet ribbon in his pocket and then, on an impulse, picked up his collection of sea glass and put it in his other pocket. He liked being able to feel the cool pieces. It was far nicer than having money in your pocket.

Miss Muggins and Harvey Angell waited for him. "Did you know," said Harvey Angell, as if he was passing the time of a very ordinary day and not ghost-watching on a rather extraordinary night, "that the word courage is a mixture of 'heart' and 'age'. Time and spirit, you might say." And he gave Henry the five hundred kilowatt beam.

"I don't know about time and spirit," said Miss Muggins, "but I'm taking my knitting. I've got quite a lot done tonight," and she held up what looked like a very long, stripy sleeve. Up in the bedroom Miss Muggins found an old bean bag and settled herself and her knitting on it.

"I'll just check the Connecting Kit," said Harvey Angell. Henry pushed up the hatch in the hidden room and the two of them crawled inside. Set up on the chest was the flowery-faced Centuries Clock and plugged into it at the back was the Energy Charger. As Harvey Angell approached, the red finger on the Charger leapt and quivered. The Clock began its familiar erratic ticking. Ten quick ticks. A long silence, then eight slow tocks and a shorter silence. In the moonlight coming through the ragged curtains, Henry saw that the fine silver fuse-wire finger of the Clock trembled just beyond the figure twenty – as if, he thought, they were only five minutes into the twentieth century.

Harvey Angell rapped the Energy Charger and checked the wiring between the two instruments. The Clock fell silent. The finger on the Energy Charger sank to zero.

"All set!" said Harvey Angell and giving Henry a final pat on the back and a flash of the five hundred kilowatt beam, he wriggled backwards out through the hatch, pulling it down behind him.

Henry was glad that although the hatch was down, the cupboard door stayed open and he could see a narrow strip of light under it. He was glad too of the pearly moonlight shining on the face of the Clock and making a puddle of light on the floor.

Henry sat in the moonlight puddle. At first the silence of the room seemed deep as time itself. Silence, Henry thought, had piled up in here its invisible sandbags of years. After a while, when his ears had adjusted to it, he could hear the comforting click of Miss Muggins' knitting needles. It was as if Miss Muggins, with her 'knit-one-pearl-one' was keeping worldly time for him while he was in this strange moonlit, timeless zone.

To calm his jumpy nerves Henry took the scarlet ribbon and the pieces of sea glass out of his pockets and laid them in the puddle of moonlight. He began making patterns. The dark blues and greens of the glass seemed to glow with a new energy. At the same moment the Clock shuddered, ticked furiously and stopped.

Then suddenly he heard her. He heard her before he saw her. It was a very muffled voice, like that of someone with her head stuck in a jersey.

"Oh! This is so . . . difficult!" said the voice. "So . . . very . . . very . . . uncomfortable. Oh! That's better!"

And there she was! Henry, immediately forgetting all about 'Good Manners for Ghosts', reached out to touch her and touched only air.

"Materialising," said the girl. "It's very difficult, very difficult indeed."

She was dressed as before with a blue pinafore over her long dress. Henry, who had imagined all ghosts to be white-faced, was surprised to see that even in the moonlight she had rosy cheeks and hair that looked newly washed.

"It's like pushing your way through very thick fog," she continued. "And I only get three goes at it. I've wasted one already and that's your fault."

"I'm terribly sorry," said Henry. Three appearances, he was thinking, like three wishes.

"Yes," said the girl, "you brought that other one, the one with the shining third eye."

"The shining third eye . . .?" echoed Henry. "Oh, you mean Mr Perkins and his torch."

"Whoever," said the girl impatiently. "It doesn't matter. Not now you're here. I've been waiting for you. Waiting ages and ages, Henry Oddity!" And with that she perched on the stool, swung her legs and grinned at him.

Even in the moonlight Henry could feel himself blushing. He hardly knew what question to ask first and then they all tumbled out at once.

"Why me? And how d'you know my name?" And, sulkily, "I hate being called Henry Oddity!"

The girl laughed. "They used to call me Lottie Oddity," she said, "so you see we're related in a way. Odd people are by far the nicest, don't you think?"

"I don't know," said Henry, who had never thought this before.

"Being odd," said Lottie, "usually means being yourself, and that's the nicest thing of all to be."

"Not if it means wearing tartan trousers," said Henry, "and being laughed at."

"It's worse being cried over," said Lottie, and for a moment a look of great sadness seemed to shadow her face. Then she smiled again. "But I like your tartan trousers," she said, "and I like you."

A kind of hot-water-bottle warmth began in Henry's stomach and spread through the rest of him. He smiled back at her. A friend was a friend – even if she was a ghost.

"But you still haven't told me how you knew my name and why you were waiting for me," he said.

"Oh we hear things on the circuit, you know," said Lottie. "It isn't all choirs of angels and bouncing on clouds. We tune in. I was told you'd be coming. But I wasn't told when. It had to be someone about my age, you see. And someone like me – a bit of an oddity. Someone who could do the mending . . ."

But before Henry could ask *what* mending, Lottie had dropped to her knees and was searching, urgently searching through the pieces of sea glass. Her smile had vanished. It was as if, Henry thought, she'd been taken over by some powerful memory from the past.

"Have you found it?" she cried, and Henry saw that her face had gone pale as if she was fading before his eyes. She reached out her hand and touched Henry's cheek and her touch was as light and cold as snow.

The memory – if a memory it was – seemed to have exhausted her. Sitting on the floor, she rocked gently backwards and forwards and Henry saw that she was now struggling to speak.

"I don't have long," she whispered. "And you have to find it before there can be any mending . . ."

Henry tried to grip her arm but grabbed only air.

"Find what? Find what?" he asked, his voice as urgent as her own.

"My Lucky, of course!" she answered. "You've got to find it. Oh why haven't you found it? I've waited so long!" And she began to sob. Lottie sobbed entirely without tears. It was strange. And sad.

"Tell me where to look! Tell me what it is!" cried Henry desperately.

"I can't! I can't! You have to make the mending. You have to work it out. And it's too late. I'm going . . . going . . ." Like her body, Lottie's voice grew fainter and fainter.

As she faded Henry heard the Centuries Clock begin a furious tick-tocking and saw that the finger of the Energy Charger had swung to 'Full Power'.

"Search! Search! Search!" he heard her say.

Then she was gone and the clock slowly subsided and the finger of the Energy Charger sank to zero.

Henry felt his own level of energy had sunk to

zero too. He could hardly heave up the hatch and crawl back into his own room.

Miss Muggins had fallen asleep on the bean bag, her knitting dropped beside her.

CHAPTER 13

It wasn't easy coming back out of the timeless zone of the hidden room into ordinary time. Crawling through the hatch, Henry felt in a kind of limbo land between the two, as if he was half asleep and half awake.

Miss Muggins was curled up asleep on the bean bag like a kitten. Henry felt as if he was seeing Miss Muggins for the first time. Had she always been so small, he wondered? Or had she shrunk? It was as if she was slowly turning into a child again. It occurred to him that he had no idea how old she was.

It seemed a shame to wake her but, after all, she was his minder and Henry felt she should be the first to know about Lottie. He knelt beside her with his face on a level with hers and shook her gently awake.

"I've seen her!" he said. "I've seen the ghost girl. Her name's Lottie."

Miss Muggins lifted her head and smiled vaguely at Henry. "That's nice, dear," she said and went back to sleep.

Maybe, thought Henry, nothing surprised you when you were very old like Miss Muggins. But then nothing surprised you when you were very young either. Henry had seen small kids at the zoo who seemed every bit as astonished by a sparrow as by a tiger. Perhaps this was what old Blake had meant when he wrote about innocence being a winter's gown. Asleep, Miss Muggins looked as innocent as a three year old. Henry found a blanket and tucked it round her. Then he drifted downstairs, still in his strange half-awake, half-asleep state.

He came to quickly enough when he got to the kitchen and four anxious, expectant faces all said, "Well?" at once.

Henry sank into a chair.

"Yes," he said, "I've seen her."

Everyone leaned forward eagerly.

"Give Henry time," said Harvey Angell, "he's got something like jet lag."

"It's very difficult materialising," said Henry.

Aunt Agatha looked alarmed. Mr Perkins felt Henry's forehead.

"Tea," said Miss Skivvy. "Hot, sweet tea. The boy's in shock."

"I'm all right," said Henry. "I'm just telling you what she said. What Lottie said."

"Lottie!" repeated Aunt Agatha. "I feel slightly better knowing she has a name."

"Being odd," said Henry dreamily, "usually means being yourself."

"And that's the nicest thing of all to be," said Harvey Angell.

Henry stared at him. Had Harvey Angell been listening at the hatch or did he have extra-sensory hearing? But Harvey Angell turned on his five hundred kilowatt beam – a particularly innocent beam this time.

Henry shook his head to try and clear his mind.

"The boy's not quite himself yet," said Aunt Agatha.

"Tell us slowly, Henry, from the beginning," said Miss Skivvy, giving Henry his mug of hot sweet tea and a whole packet of biscuits. (A *whole* packet made Henry feel rather heroic. And Aunt Agatha didn't even blink!) But somehow, perhaps because it was so late or perhaps because the night was so like a dream, Henry's meeting with Lottie didn't seem to have a beginning, middle and end. It felt all of a piece.

"She was waiting for me," said Henry. "She's been waiting for ages."

"Ah! Just as I thought," murmured Harvey Angell. "A ghost often needs a kind of kindred spirit."

"What's a kindred spirit?" asked Henry.

"A sort of special friend," said Harvey Angell. "Someone you're related to – not by blood like a brother or sister, but by heart."

It was Henry's turn to beam.

"I think Blake's my kindred spirit," said Mr Perkins.

"Let's keep Blake out of this," said Aunt Agatha, giving Mr Perkins one of her old and most withering looks. "I'd really like to get some sleep tonight. Henry, would you please tell us about this ghost child – this Lottie. Who is she? What did she say? What does she want?"

But before Henry could attempt an answer, Miss Skivvy had leapt up from the table. "Muggins!" she cried. "Where's Muggins? What if the ghost child's stolen Muggins?"

Henry noticed that though dressed in her nightie, Miss Skivvy was still wearing her orange armbands. It made her look as if she was trying to grow wings. It was odd. It was nice. It was very Miss Skivvy.

"It's all right," he said, "Miss Muggins is asleep on the bean bag. I gave her a blanket." Now that he'd finished his tea and was half way through the packet of biscuits he was beginning to feel more himself. More in time. Present time.

"Let Miss Muggins sleep," said Harvey Angell. "And there's no need for me to keep watch. The child – Lottie – won't appear twice on the same night."

"She said she was only allowed three goes," said Henry through a mouthful of biscuit. "Three goes at – at materialising." He said the word carefully. It was a nice, long, slow word. He spread it out like margarine on a slice of bread – mat-eeeer-real-eyes-iiiing. Yes, that was how Lottie had appeared. And disappeared.

"Ah! Three!" said Harvey Angell. "Once for a last look back, twice for a message or request, three times for unfinished business. That'll be it. I suppose you didn't happen to notice where the finger of the Centuries Clock was pointing, did you, Henry?"

"Of course I did," said Henry proudly. "It was seven minutes past twenty."

"It all fits," said Harvey Angell.

Aunt Agatha banged a teaspoon on the table. "It might all fit to you," she said, "but nothing's making much sense to me. What does seven minutes past twenty mean? And I'm still waiting for Henry to tell me why this child is haunting Sibbald House. For the last time, Henry, why is she here and what does she *want*?"

"She wants me to find her Lucky," said Henry.

"I shouldn't think she had much of that," said Miss Skivvy. "Luck, I mean."

"Oh I don't know," said Mr Perkins. "I should quite like to be a ghost . . . one day."

"But not quite now," said Miss Skivvy.

"No," agreed Mr Perkins. "Not quite now."

"And," Henry plunged on for the dreamy feeling was clearing, like mist, and the encounter with Lottie was now bright and sharp in his mind, "there's some mending to do."

"Oh yes," said Harvey Angell. "Mending the connections."

"But *what* connections?" asked Aunt Agatha. "And what or where is the child's Lucky?"

"I don't know," said Henry. "But I'm going to look," he added fiercely. "I'm going to look and look and look till I find it."

"Seven minutes past twenty," said Mr Perkins. "We haven't heard what that means."

"Probably about 1927," said Harvey Angell. "Every five minutes on the Centuries Clock equals ten years."

"Was that when Lottie was born?" asked Henry.

"More likely when she died," said Harvey Angell.

"Well, I suppose that's something like a fact," said Aunt Agatha, "though I don't see it helps us much. Henry, is that *all* you can tell us?"

"Yes," said Henry miserably, for what he had told them sounded so little and felt so big. There were things he couldn't explain. The strange feeling he'd had of being in another time zone. The words to tell how sad he'd felt seeing Lottie sob without tears. The hot-water-bottle warmth of finding a friend – even a ghost friend. And the way, crawling back through the hatch into present time, he'd felt he too was 'materialising'. Henry Oddity, his own true self.

"To sum up," said Aunt Agatha, as if she wanted everything as neat and tidy as her accounts book, "all we know is that the ghost child's name is Lottie, that she died around 1927, that she wants Henry to find her Lucky – whatever that may be – and something or other needs mending."

"And she can only appear one more time," added Mr Perkins.

"Sleep," said Aunt Agatha. "We all need sleep. Tomorrow morning will be time enough to start looking for Lottie's Lucky."

"If no one minds, I think I'll carry on playing my flute," said Harvey Angell. "I'm not at all tired."

And nobody did mind, for Harvey Angell's music was the sort that wove in and out of your dreams.

"Sometimes," said Harvey Angell, as Henry climbed wearily upstairs, "music can say what words can't."

In bed and in the few minutes before he fell asleep, Henry listened to the song of the flute. The song was like the pearly moonlight in Lottie's room; it wove in and out of time. For a while Henry tried to follow the melody but it led him this way and that, and soon he was lost in it. The song seemed to take him travelling in time. The notes drifted through the house in such a haunting way that Henry wondered if, somewhere, somewhere on the circuit, Lottie – Lottie Oddity, as he secretly called her to himself – could hear it too.

Chapter 13

How *odd*, was Henry's last thought before he slept, that the word 'oddity' sounded very like 'jollity'. He would have to tell Mr Perkins this in the morning. Perhaps Mr Perkins could use it in a poem.

CHAPTER 14

Henry woke up knowing there were two very important things he had to do that day – search for Lottie's Lucky and see if Tom Troone was back. There were questions Henry desperately wanted to ask the old man.

But downstairs Henry found Harvey Angell in the hall, putting on his helicopter helmet. Henry's heart sank to his sandals.

"You're not going, are you?" he asked. "Not now. Not yet. Not before we've found the Lucky!"

"Had a message last night," said Harvey Angell, picking up his tool bag. "Got a little Homing work to do."

It was on the tip of Henry's tongue to ask *how* the message had come and if it was the letter they'd sent to the Waifs and Strays Café that had brought him to Sibbald House or if (as Henry half suspected) writing 'HARVEY ANGELL' in the sand had done it. But again Harvey Angell gave him a full-strength beam and the question melted in Henry's head like an ice-lolly in the sun.

"Don't worry," said Harvey Angell. "I'll be back tonight."

"But how will I find Lottie's Lucky without you?" asked Henry. "And what d'you think it could be?"

"I haven't the least idea," said Harvey Angell cheerfully. "But you'll know it when you find it."

There wasn't much comfort in *that*, thought Henry, following Harvey Angell outside. It was a shining morning. The sort of morning you never see in the city. Sky, rocks, cliffs, clouds all looked as if they'd been in the washing machine overnight.

Henry stood by the sea wall and watched Harvey Angell climb into his helicopter. Soon the rotor blades were whirling, spinning the morning sunshine into sparkling dust. The seagulls, perched on their usual strand of rock, took off as the engine came to life. For a moment it looked as if the helicopter hung under a white parachute of gulls, as if they were its escort. Then the gulls streamed seawards and the helicopter flew high over the cliffs. Henry watched it growing smaller and smaller until it looked no larger than a dragonfly. When it was out of sight he went miserably back into Sibbald House.

Aunt Agatha had thrown all the windows open. It was something Henry remembered her doing on New Year's Eve when, she told him, it was to let the old year out and the new year in. Despite the sunniness of the day, Henry had the odd feeling that he wanted to close them all, to keep Lottie safe until he had found her Lucky. But he said nothing.

Mr Perkins was finishing his breakfast, a book propped up against the sugar bowl. The title, Henry saw, was *Sea Witch*. Why on earth did Mr Perkins want a story about a sea witch when Sibbald House had its own story? A real-life story. A story in which Mr Perkins had a part.

Mr Perkins looked over the top of his book at Henry, smoothed his wisps and grinned. "Sometimes I think I like made-up stories better than real ones," he said. "And sometimes I'm not sure I can tell the difference." And he went back to his book.

Aunt Agatha was doing her holiday accounts. (She had a special notebook for them.) Miss Skivvy and Miss Muggins were packing a picnic. Henry sat down at the table and helped himself to cereal. Really, he thought, anyone would think this was a perfectly ordinary holiday day and not the morning after he'd seen a ghost. Suddenly he felt very alone.

"I thought you were all going to help me look," he said. "Look for the Lucky."

"Muggins and I have other plans," said Miss Skivvy, putting two apples and two packets of crisps into the picnic basket. "We're off to the beach."

"The thing is," said Mr Perkins as gently as he could, "we've talked this through, Henry, and we feel that the ghost child – Lottie – appeared to you. It was you she was waiting for. I'm not sure we can be much help."

"Oh," said Henry, stirring his cornflakes which seemed to have gone as soggy as his hopes.

"And I don't see how you can find something when you don't know what you're looking for," said Aunt Agatha.

"That's no reason not to look," said Henry fiercely.

"Henry's absolutely right!" said Aunt Agatha, slapping the accounts book on the table. "Let's start now. Perkins! Stop hiding in a book. We'll begin at the top of the house and work down."

* * *

They spent all morning looking. The house, which had seemed so empty, so sparsely furnished, when they'd arrived, seemed to have grown cupboards and corners, nooks and crannies, not to mention various loose floorboards under which someone – Lottie – might have hidden something precious, something lucky.

Opening a drawer in the kitchen, Henry found an old fishing net stiff with salt and two knives with broken handles. In a corner cupboard of the sitting room, Aunt Agatha found three baskets, an old apron, a skein of wool that had lost its colour and a sack. Mr Perkins found one old black leather boot.

In his own bedroom Henry found two marbles, a tin of rusty nails and a cup without a handle. There was nothing here that anyone might think precious or special. Nothing that looked remotely like a lucky talisman or charm. Nothing gold. Nothing silver. Nothing that looked loved and lucky.

Between them, by lunch time, they'd found a great deal of useless junk and a great deal of dust.

"Well," said Aunt Agatha, "at least I've cleared out a lot of cupboards. I reckon Tom Troone should give us a discount on the rent for all this cleaning."

"I'm going to see if Tom Troone's home," said Henry. He hadn't planned to say this. It came out like a decision he'd made ages ago. In his sleep, perhaps. Or even when he was 'materialising' through the hatch out of time past and into time present. There was no 'can I?' attached to it. Back in the city there was hardly anywhere – apart from school – where Henry was allowed to go alone. Now he waited for Aunt Agatha's usual, "No, Henry, I don't think that's a good idea."

But it didn't come. Aunt Agatha seemed to be studying him very carefully. Then she swept the lunch dishes into the sink and said, "Yes, Henry, if Tom Troone is home I think he's more likely to talk to you than he is to me. Best go on your own. You can bring me a bag of potatoes on your way back."

Henry felt rather put out. He hadn't wanted Aunt Agatha to agree so easily. His brief moment of courage faded when he remembered how scared of Tom Troone he'd felt on that first stormy night. He would have liked a little tut-tutting from Aunt Agatha or Mr Perkins. An 'Are you sure you can manage on your own, dear? And will you be all right?' But apparently all Aunt Agatha could think of was potatoes! Henry slammed the door behind him and moodily set off up the sea road. There was no sign of Miss Skivvy or Miss Muggins on the beach. Where had they got to?

How odd grown-ups were, he thought. About the little things of life, about things like bedtime and potatoes, they seemed to care a great deal. But about the important, urgent things – like finding Lottie's Lucky or mending the connections – they were curiously casual. Harvey Angell wasn't like that, thought Henry. In some ways Harvey Angell seemed years and years and years old. And at the same time he seemed just about the same age as Henry himself.

As he reached the harbour road he saw a fishing boat coming in. He stopped to watch it. Like Harvey Angell's helicopter, it was accompanied by a riot of seagulls, blowing about it like a windblown flag. Henry gazed out to sea. You could see on and on and on, into forever, he thought. Once upon a time Lottie must have stood just here and looked out to sea as he was looking now. The thought made Henry shiver. For a moment longer he stood watching the boat turn into the harbour and the men on board unwinding the rope ready to sling it to land, then he turned and headed for Cove Wynd and Tom Troone.

But when he reached Tom Troone's cottage he was disappointed again. The curtains were still drawn and although he knocked on the door, somehow he knew, by the stillness of the place, that there was no one home. The silence sank his heart. Even a very angry Tom Troone would be better than the blank eyes-shut face of the cottage. It began to feel like a day when nothing was going to go right. An *unlucky* day. A day when his courage felt wasted. I wouldn't be surprised, Henry said to himself, stomping down the Wynd, if there were no potatoes in the Harbour Stores.

Mrs MacReadie was sitting outside the Stores again, perched on her stool and with another sleeve of purple knitting. She was looking cheerful and friendly as if she'd forgotten their questions about Tom Troone. She patted a spare stool beside her and Henry sat down.

"On your own today?" she asked.

"Yes," said Henry. (He didn't dare mention Tom Troone's name again.)

"I suppose you're a city lad," said Mrs MacReadie. "Sometimes I've wanted to live in a city. But I was born and bred here and I'll not leave it now."

It was nice sitting in the sunshine of the harbour. It made Henry feel as if he too belonged to the place. At least for the moment he could pretend. He looked at the fishing boat he'd watched coming in. With its many wires and its huge winch it looked like a floating factory. Lottie, he thought, would have been amazed to see it.

"What was it like here, years and years ago?" he asked.

Mrs MacReadie gave him a sideways glance. "Well I'm not that old," she said. "How many years ago did you have in mind?"

"Well, maybe when you were about my age," said Henry.

"I was not much older than you when I was a fisher-lassie," said Mrs MacReadie.

"You went to sea? You went fishing?" said Henry.

"Oh no! Not us lassies," said Mrs MacReadie, laughing. "That was for the men. Our job was packing and salting the herring. And hard work it was too. Me and my sister, we used to bandage our hands when we were gutting the fish to try and stop the salt getting into the wounds. You couldn't help but cut yourself, see. But you always had the company of the other lassies. *And* you got to travel."

"But I thought you stayed ashore while the men went to sea?" said Henry.

"We followed the herring fleet, you see," said Mrs MacReadie. Her knitting had fallen in her lap and she looked out into the harbour as if she could still see the fleet. "My sister and I went to the Shetlands. And Wick and Frazeborough. Then round about August we'd go south. Places like Yarmouth and Lowestoft."

Mrs MacReadie picked up her knitting. "But none of that lasted long after the war when they gave up on steam boats and started using diesel and they had these great big nets that took all the fish before they were fully grown. And then all those fish and chip shops!" There was an angry note in Mrs MacReadie's voice now.

"Fish and chip shops?" asked Henry. He'd been dreaming about Lottie. Wondering if she'd been a fisher-lassie with bandages on her cut hands. If she'd travelled to Shetland and Wick, Yarmouth and Lowestoft.

"Who wanted herrings when they could have cheap white fish ready cooked in batter?" asked Mrs Mac-Readie. "Herring went out of fashion. I doubt you've ever eaten one, have you?"

Henry had to admit he hadn't. But it wasn't herring or fish and chip shops he wanted to talk about now. He'd had a sudden brain wave. He tried to ask the question casually, but it burst out of him.

"Did you – did you ever know a girl called Lottie?" he asked.

At once Mrs MacReadie was off her stool, snapping her knitting needles together and marching back into the Stores.

"I can't be sitting round here talking to you all day," she said. "I've things to do. Were you wanting anything?" And once again her face – like Tom Troone's cottage – was closed up.

"Potatoes," said Henry glumly. "I want a bag of potatoes."

Just as glumly, Henry humped the potatoes back to Sibbald House. He had a horrible sense of failure, as if he'd shrunk at least six inches. He'd wanted a holiday adventure, hadn't he? Well, he'd got one. And what had he done with it? Nothing! Lottie, Lottie Oddity, his friend, needed him – trusted him – to find her Lucky and he hadn't found it. What if she returned that night – materialising for the third and final time? Would she be miserably stuck on 'the circuit', the circuit between the living and the dead? Stuck forever haunting Sibbald House, wanting her Lucky, unable to mend the connections? It didn't bear thinking about.

Then there was Tom Troone. Henry felt sure Tom Troone knew that Sibbald House was haunted by a child. Why else had his advertisement said 'Child essential'? I bet he thought a live child might free the house of the ghost child, Henry said to himself. And it would happen just like that. Pffff! And she'd be gone. If only he knew more about Lottie then perhaps he could find her Lucky and Tom Troone – if and when he ever came home – was the only one who could help.

And what about Harvey Angell? What was he up to? Henry examined the sky, hoping to see the helicopter, but the sky was as blank and silent as Tom Troone's empty house. Henry felt that his head was full of questions and there was no answer to any of them. No reply. What was it Harvey Angell had said – it takes time to make the connections. Well, there was only one week left of the holiday. Was that time enough?

"Watts and volts, watts and volts,
Better by far than thunderbolts,"

Henry chanted, dumping the bag of potatoes on the kitchen table. Well, right now he wouldn't mind a quick thunderbolt.

★ ★ ★

Up the High Street in The Cosy Kettle Tea Rooms, Miss Muggins and Miss Skivvy shared a pot of tea and a large piece of chocolate cake.

"I don't plan to spend the rest of this holiday baby-sitting a ghost," said Miss Skivvy. "What we need is a few facts."

"A gossip with the locals," said Miss Muggins.

"Exactly," said Miss Skivvy.

"There's a Women's Institute market tomorrow morning," said Miss Muggins.

"Perfect," said Miss Skivvy. "I wonder if Harvey Angell could use our services from time to time?"

"You mean sort of background research?" said Miss Muggins.

"Yes," said Miss Skivvy, finishing the chocolate cake. "We could set up a nice little business. Skivvy and Muggins, ghost busters."

CHAPTER 15

That night Henry found it impossible to sleep. It was listening that kept him awake. Listening for Lottie. Listening for Harvey Angell. All he could hear was Mr Perkins snoring.

There was a rhythm to Mr Perkins' snores. They went, 'Phut phut hup! Phut phut hup!' Then there was a long silence and Henry was just about to fall asleep when they started up again, 'Phut phut hup! Phut phut hup!'

Of course Henry was glad not to be alone in the room with the hatch, but he began to wish he was back in his attic in Ballantyre Road, snug in his own comfortable bed and with the familiar noises of late-night traffic to soothe him to sleep. The mattress he now tossed and turned on felt as if it was full of stones.

When, in between Mr Perkins' phuts and hups, Henry fell into a doze, he dreamt of Lottie. In his dream she was first a fisher-lassie carrying a large basket of herrings on her hip. Next he saw her dancing on the beach, the red ribbon flying in her hair. Three boys followed behind her, taunting,

"Lottie Oddity! Lottie Oddity!" Then he saw the tide rush in and heard her cry out. A single, long scream. He woke with a start and looked at his watch. Two in the morning and still no Harvey Angell.

Henry got out of bed and crept out of the room. Somehow the house, without Harvey Angell in it, seemed chilly as if, like Lottie, it was stuck in a cold winter and no amount of sunshine could warm it.

Henry stopped on the landing and looked out of the window. The tide was far out and there was only a sliver of a moon. He was just about to go downstairs and get himself a drink and maybe a comfort biscuit when what he saw through the window glued him there.

There was a a figure on the beach! A man's figure, stooped under a haversack and walking slowly towards the harbour. Despite the darkness Henry recognised him at once. It was Tom Troone! Henry had to stop himself from shouting out loud and hammering on the window. He watched the old man turn off towards Cove Wynd. Should he follow him now? Or wait until morning?

Before he could decide he heard a noise like the throb of a metal washboard, faint at first and then getting louder and louder until it was throbbing over the house. Then he saw it – Harvey Angell's helicopter – a light brilliant as a star at its tail, circling, circling over the beach and finally dropping neatly down on its ski-like feet.

Henry ran downstairs, flung open the door and in bare feet and jumble pyjamas (yellow stripe) raced down to the beach.

"Hello, Henry," said Harvey Angell, as if he wasn't

a bit surprised to find Henry awake and on the beach in the middle of the night. "Lovely night, isn't it?"

And Henry, who had been far too anxious and jittery to notice, suddenly saw that it was. The night was soft and balmy and full of stars.

"Tom Troone!" gasped Henry. "I've just seen him! Did you bring him back?"

"I may have helped," said Harvey Angell, "but it's more likely that Lottie brought him back. And you, Henry."

"Lottie? Me? I don't understand!" Henry cried, jumping up and down with impatience.

Harvey Angell took off his helmet and reached for his tool bag.

"Here, carry this," he said. "Did Aunt Agatha buy any cocoa? I could just do with a mug or five. And by the look of it, so could you."

* * *

"So what did you mean?" asked Henry when they were in the kitchen drinking cocoa. "About it being Lottie or me who brought Tom Troone home? You must have found him."

"Well, yes," admitted Harvey Angell. "Finding him was the easy part. A man like Tom Troone would keep close to the sea, wouldn't he? All I had to do was follow the coast road."

"But you arrived almost together . . ." said Henry.

"That's easy to explain," said Harvey Angell. "I found him soon after I set out this morning. Spent most of the day giving him the nudge. Then I had other things to do. We Homers, you know, we've got more calls to make than your family GP, and then there were the messages . . ." Harvey Angell stretched and yawned.

"But what did you *do*?" Henry interrupted. "It must have been a very big nudge – more a kind of push – to make him come home."

Harvey Angell grinned. He took the silver flute from the pocket of his dungarees and played a snatch of a tune. At once Henry felt such an urgent longing to be home in Ballantyre Road that his eyes stung with tears. Harvey Angell stopped playing and the longing faded with the tune.

"It's 'O That I'm Longing for my Ain Folk'," said Harvey Angell. "A real winner. The Homer's Homesick Song. Never fails! You see I've been busking, Henry, like your Aunt Agatha."

"No, I don't see," said Henry.

"Well, once I'd found Tom Troone I followed him. And once I'd realised he was following the coast road I could use the helicopter to get ahead of him. Whenever he turned up in a new village, there I was, playing the Homesick Song. I think I've busked on all the beaches in Fife by now. And in all the small cafés."

"But where's he been sleeping?" asked Henry. "And why couldn't you just introduce yourself and ask him about Lottie and Sibbald House?"

"Tom Troone's got a tent, of course," said Harvey Angell, "and I couldn't do what you suggest because it's not the Homer's way."

Henry sighed. "What *is* the Homer's way?" he asked.

"A Homer," said Harvey Angell, leaning his elbows on the table and giving Henry the full beam, "can clear the lines – the lines between the past and the present, lines that get clogged with sadness – "

"Tom Troone's more angry than sad," Henry interrupted.

"Sadness in disguise," said Harvey Angell. "As I was saying, we Homers can clear the lines, but the Energy – the love that mends the connections – that has to come from you . . ."

"From Lottie and me?" asked Henry.

"Yes. And Tom Troone too, I think," said Harvey Angell. "Something happened to Tom Troone long ago that froze his heart. All I know is that we need him. And Lottie needs him. I might have nudged him home but I think he's still switched off . . ."

"Like Aunt Agatha was by a sorrow she didn't want to think about," said Henry, remembering how things had been at 131 Ballantyre Road before Harvey Angell had arrived.

"Yes," said Harvey Angell. "I think I got to Ballantyre Road just in time. It might be too late for Tom Troone."

"We *can't* be too late!" cried Henry. "For Lottie's sake we can't."

"I always forget," said Harvey Angell, "what a short-sighted view of time people have. Why, some jobs have taken me centuries to complete! Just because you don't finish something, Henry, doesn't mean someone else won't finish it for you. Eventually."

"I don't care about centuries and eventually," said Henry fiercely. "I've got one week of this holiday left."

"We'll have to see what we can do then, won't we?" said Harvey Angell. "In the morning you can go round to Tom Troone's. See if he'll talk. Right now we both need some sleep."

It was Henry's turn to yawn. It *had* been an unlucky day, he decided, when he was back in bed and trying to find a comfortable hollow in the lumpy mattress, but now that Harvey Angell was back, that would change. Tomorrow he'd look for Lottie's Lucky again – *and* talk to Tom Troone. And somehow with Harvey Angell asleep in the room with the hatch, the room next to Lottie's, it was easy to sleep.

"Phut phut hup!" snored Mr Perkins, but Henry no longer heard him.

CHAPTER 16

Henry put on clean jeans and his quietest T-shirt. "Your hair, Henry," said Aunt Agatha. "When did it last see a brush?"

Henry had a strong feeling that Tom Troone wouldn't care about clean clothes and brushed hair, but he brushed it all the same. It was like going for an interview with the headmaster, he thought, looking at himself in the hall mirror. Only worse. At least you knew the headmaster would talk to you.

Miss Muggins and Miss Skivvy were also in the hall, trying on hats. They were going to the WI market, they said. Miss Muggins had borrowed Mr Perkins' cap and pinned flowers on its peak. Miss Skivvy had collected gulls' feathers and stuck them in her straw hat so that she looked vaguely like an Indian squaw gone wrong. (Her skateboard was at the ready.)

Aunt Agatha and Mr Perkins sat on the stairs watching.

"You'll certainly make an entrance in those hats!" said Aunt Agatha.

"That's just what we want," said Miss Skivvy.

"We want to be noticed," said Miss Muggins, "so everyone will talk to us."

"That will do, Muggins," said Miss Skivvy, digging Miss Muggins in the ribs with her bony elbow.

"I think you look very nice," said Henry loyally.

"And so do you, Henry," said Miss Muggins. "I'm sure Mr Troone will be very pleased to see a nice young man like you. Why don't you take him an ice-cream cornet?"

"Or a poem," said Mr Perkins. "I'm sure I could find a poem about a haunted house. How about,

'Is there anyone there?' said the Traveller,
Knocking on the moonlit door . . .'"

Aunt Agatha clapped her hands in exasperation. "Henry will just take himself," she said, "though why Mr Angell won't let me go too, I don't know. I'd like to give that Mr Troone a piece of my mind – renting us a haunted house. *He* should be paying *us*!"

"Whenever I give someone a piece of my mind it always seems to fly back at me like a boomerang," said Mr Perkins thoughtfully.

"Probably because there aren't many useful thoughts in your mind, Perkins," said Aunt Agatha crisply. "It's too cluttered up with poems."

"Yes dear," said Mr Perkins sadly.

"Where *is* Harvey Angell?" asked Henry.

"Doing his sun salutations," said Aunt Agatha.

"For the Energy," said Mr Perkins.

Henry looked puzzled.

"On the beach," said Aunt Agatha. "You'll see him on your way. Miss Skivvy, do you really need *all* those feathers? And if you go on that skateboard I doubt anyone will talk to you! I hope you are not planning to spend a lot of money on extras like cakes."

"We're after clues . . . I mean bargains," said Miss Muggins.

"I'm not too sure you haven't both got sunstroke," said Aunt Agatha. "In fact I'm beginning to think that holidays are not good for people."

Henry went out of the house grinning. But his grin didn't last long. As soon as he was outside, all his fear of Tom Troone returned. He looked about the beach for Harvey Angell. Some last-minute advice might help. Sun salutations, thought Henry, half expecting to see Harvey Angell perched on a rock and waving to the sun.

But Harvey Angell was on the beach, standing on his head. Was he saluting the sun 'down under' in Australia? Or waving at it with his feet, wondered Henry? As he watched, Harvey Angell leapt upright again, bowed three times and was balanced on his head again. Perhaps head-stands were necessary to Homers. Maybe it gave them a different view of the world. Or jiggled their brains. Henry ran down on to the beach.

"Sorry to interrupt," he said, kneeling beside the upside-down Harvey Angell so as to talk to him face to face.

"Quite all right," said Harvey Angell. "I'm just having breakfast."

"Breakfast?"

"Sea air. Sunshine. Energy," said Harvey Angell, bouncing upright again. "Much better for you than cereal or bacon and eggs."

"I suppose so," said Henry doubtfully, thinking that sea air and sunshine didn't quite fill you up like cereal, bacon and eggs did. "I just wondered if you had any advice," he said. "About Tom Troone, I mean, and the best way to approach him."

"Smile," said Harvey Angell, turning the right way up and sitting neatly in the lotus position.

"Ummm," said Henry. But my smile isn't like your smile, he wanted to say. It was true that Miss Muggins had often told him that he had a very nice smile, but Henry knew it was an ordinary sort of smile. It wasn't a smile that dazzled thoughts out of people's heads or made them feel suddenly warm. Henry's smile didn't have Angell magic.

All the same, he practised smiling as he made his way up the Harbour Road and towards Cove Wynd. And in between smiles he tried to rehearse what he might say to Tom Troone. In bed, the night before, he'd had a picture of himself and Tom Troone – now a mellow, kindly and above all *welcoming* Tom Troone – chatting on either side of the fire, and Tom Troone telling him *everything* . . . whatever everything was.

Suddenly it all seemed rather more difficult than that and the main difficulty was how to begin. Henry tried out a few opening lines. "Good morning, Mr Troone, I've come about Lottie . . ." But did Tom Troone know the ghost child's name was Lottie? What exactly *did* he know?

Henry tried again. "Good morning, Mr Troone. I'm sorry to disturb you, but it's about the ghost at Sibbald House . . ." This was even worse. Tom Troone might well think he was mad. Well, let him, thought Henry defiantly, and putting his hands on his hips he tried: "We know you know about the ghost child, Mr Troone . . ." That sounded like the police, thought Henry, about to make an arrest.

And then he was standing in front of Tom Troone's cottage with his hand lifted to knock on the knocker and a smile which, try as he might, wouldn't stay stuck on his face.

The Tom Troone who opened the door an inch and peered out at Henry was a very different Tom Troone from the fearsome, angry giant Henry had met on that first night of the holiday. Henry remembered how then the old man had reminded him of the Seafarer, 'clenched against clinging sorrow'. Tom Troone seemed to have worn himself to the bone with all that walking. Was he more bent? Had his sea-blue eyes faded? Henry wasn't sure, but he heard himself saying in a very small voice, "Excuse me, Mr Troone, but . . ."

"Has she gone?" whispered Tom Troone. "Our Lottie. Has she gone?"

"So you do know who she is!" cried Henry.

"Know who she is? I wish to God I didn't!" said the old man. "But is she still there?"

"Oh yes," said Henry eagerly. "If I could come in, sir, I'll tell you about her. You see, what she wants is – "

But Tom Troone didn't give him the chance to finish his sentence.

"Then she hasn't forgiven me!" he groaned and slammed the door in Henry's face.

"But Mr Troone! Mr Troone!" called Henry and he beat on the door with his fist and shouted through the letter box.

It was no use. Tom Troone clearly had no intention of opening the door again. And Henry found himself running back down the Wynd blinded by tears. Angry tears. It was all so silly! Why should he care? He'd come as a stranger to Sibbald House. Lottie was not his problem.

But she was! Oh she was! You couldn't come upon an accident in the street and say it wasn't your problem. You were there. And Lottie was more than that. She was his first real friend. It didn't matter that she'd lived in another time and another place. She was the first person he'd met who knew what it felt like to be the odd-one-out. And more importantly, she'd made Henry feel less like an 'oddity' and more like himself. A far happier self.

Henry ran all the way back to Sibbald House. There was a note on the door in Aunt Agatha's writing. 'Gone to the beach,' it read. 'Key under mat.' Henry let himself in. He went into the sitting room and flopped on to the mouldy sofa. Best control his tears before going down to the beach. But within minutes, exhausted by his sleepless night and his fears about Tom Troone, he was fast asleep.

* * *

The WI market, held in the church hall, was buzzing with eager shoppers. Trestle tables had been set up, loaded with cakes and biscuits, plants and flowers, hand-knitted socks and baby clothes, jars of jams and marmalades.

"We'll start at one end and work down to the other," said Miss Skivvy. "Have you remembered your lines, Muggins?"

"Yes," said Miss Muggins. "I say, 'What a lovely market. I'm on holiday here . . .' "

"And they say . . .?"

" 'How nice. Where are you staying?' And I say, 'Sibbald House. It's a very interesting house, I wonder if you know anything about its history?' "

"You've got it," said Miss Skivvy. "Now try to look happy, Muggins, and if you want to write down any clues, pretend it's your shopping list."

"Right," said Miss Muggins, getting out a small notebook.

But finding out about Sibbald House proved harder than they'd imagined. Very soon they'd bought one jar of damson jam, one of marmalade, a large spider plant and a banoffie tart – and had drawn a blank.

"How nice! I hope you have a lovely holiday," said the woman on the plant stall when Miss Muggins made her opening speech.

"Don't you want to know where I'm staying?" asked Miss Muggins.

"Not really, dear. That'll be one pound forty, please."

Miss Skivvy did a little better. Three times she got as far as asking about the history of Sibbald House.

"You'll be finding it very strange there," said the woman on the knitwear stall. But as soon as Miss Skivvy tried to ask more questions, the woman turned away.

"A very troubled house," said the woman on the home-made bread stall. "They never got over the loss, you know."

But just as Miss Skivvy was about to launch into a lot of questions beginning with who, why and what, the woman patted her arm and said, "It's something we prefer not to talk about."

At the last stall of all – the Home Bakes stall, attended by a woman with three pairs of spectacles, one on her head, one on a chain round her neck and the third on her nose – they struck lucky.

"Ah," said the woman when Miss Muggins repeated her speech about Sibbald House (which now came out very fast), "a sad house, that one. A very sad house." She swopped the spectacles on her head for the ones on her nose. "What about this lemon meringue pie?"

"We'll have it," said Miss Skivvy quickly. "How do you mean, sad?"

"Why, on account of the child that was drowned," said the woman. "Now these scones are lovely. I baked them this morning."

"Yes," said Miss Skivvy. "Put them in. What do you know about her – this child?"

"Lottie, I think her name was. Tom Troone's sister, you know." (Miss Skivvy and Miss Muggins exchanged triumphant glances.) "And how about this nice pot of strawberry jam to go with the scones?"

"Yes, yes, yes," said Miss Skivvy. "And how did it happen?"

"Well, she went out fishing with her father. Baggsy should have gone . . ."

"Baggsy?"

"That's what we used to call Tom Troone. On account of him always wearing baggy trousers. Well, he should have gone, but Lottie went in his place. They both drowned, father and daughter. Now this shortbread would make a lovely present to take home with you . . ."

"Scrumptious. We'll take it," said Miss Skivvy.

"Well, old Tom, he never got over it," said the

woman, adding the shortbread to the bulging carrier bag and changing spectacles again. "Goes off walking twice a year. Once on her birthday and once on the anniversary of her death." She leaned over the table. "Sibbald House is where they used to live, you know. They say it's been haunted ever since and that she drove him out . . . Have you perhaps seen . . . anyone?"

"I think that will be all, thank you," said Miss Skivvy, giving Miss Muggins a push towards the door. "You've been very helpful. Very helpful indeed."

Outside the church hall Miss Skivvy and Miss Muggins shook hands.

"Muggins," said Miss Skivvy, "I think we've cracked it."

* * *

It was habit that made Henry slide his hand down the side of the mouldy sofa. Down the sides of the sofa in Ballantyre Road (old but not mouldy) Henry often found lost things – biros, two pence pieces, half a biscuit. Now, when he woke up, he automatically did the same thing, squeezing his fingers down the side of the sofa and finding, at first, a good deal of dust and grit.

Then he felt it. Something cold and hard. And stuck. He tried to work out what it was from its shape and feel, but couldn't. He knelt on the sofa, pushed his hand down and with two fingers tried to loosen the object and prise it up. It shifted slowly until, holding it between finger and thumb and scraping his knuckles on the hard wooden side of the sofa, he pulled it slowly out.

Chapter 16

It was a piece of sea glass. But the most beautiful piece Henry had ever seen! Beside it, the pieces he'd collected himself were just pale fragments. This sea glass was chunky as a big diamond. It was a deep, dark blue as if it had come from the deepest, bluest part of the ocean and had been worn smooth by centuries of rolling tides.

Henry jumped off the sofa and held the sea glass up to the light. It shone as if the sea was caught inside it. And then Henry knew. Knew without doubt that he'd found it. Lottie's Lucky!

CHAPTER 17

Henry almost knocked Miss Skivvy off her skate-board as he dashed out of the house clutching the sea glass. Behind Miss Skivvy he could see Miss Muggins struggling along with two large carrier bags, a spider plant thrusting its fronds out of one of them. But he couldn't wait. He ran for the beach shouting, "I've found it! I've found it!"

Aunt Agatha and Mr Perkins had both fallen asleep in the mid-day sun – Aunt Agatha in the deck-chair, Mr Perkins on a rug at her feet. They woke together looking startled. Harvey Angell appeared to be writing names in a circle on the sand.

"I've found it!" Henry repeated as they all gaped at him. "Lottie's Lucky. I've found it!" And he stretched out his hand with the sea glass hidden in his closed fist.

"Is it a gold coin?" asked Aunt Agatha hopefully.

"An emerald?" said Mr Perkins. "Emeralds mean 'Success in Love'." He gazed wistfully at Aunt Agatha.

"They mean a lot of money," said Aunt Agatha. "Show us, Henry! Show us!"

Henry opened his fist and the sea glass lay on his palm, glowing.

There was a long silence. Aunt Agatha heaved a sigh.

"Not worth a bean," she said. "But very beautiful," and she gave Henry a hug.

"Full of the North Sea," said Harvey Angell. "No wonder she missed it. Well done, Henry."

"It was down the side of the sofa," said Henry.

"Funny how people forget to look in the most obvious places," said Harvey Angell.

"I shall write an ode about it," said Mr Perkins solemnly.

"And did you see Tom Troone, Henry?" Aunt Agatha asked.

Henry's face clouded over. "He wouldn't see me," he said. "He knows about Lottie. But he wants her to go away. When I told him I'd seen her he said, 'Then she's not forgiven me' and shut the door in my face."

"That's a great pity," said Harvey Angell. "Without Tom Troone I doubt we can free Sibbald House of sorrow."

"But we've got Lottie's Lucky now," said Henry. "All I've got to do is give it to her. I'm sure if I put it in her room – on her dressing table perhaps – she'll appear again. And once she has the sea glass she'll be free, won't she? Free to go off – on the circuit."

"You're forgetting the mending that needs to be done," said Harvey Angell. "Mending the connections. Finding the sea glass is just the beginning . . ." But before he could say more, Miss Skivvy and Miss Muggins came hurrying down to the beach. They were both red in the face. The feathers in Miss

Skivvy's hat were sticking out wildly and a limp poppy drooped from Miss Muggins' cap.

"What on earth have you two been doing?" demanded Aunt Agatha, trying to look very upright, which wasn't easy in a deck-chair. "You look as if you've been on the big dipper in Blackpool."

"Well, something just as exciting," said Miss Skivvy.

"Henry's found Lottie's Lucky," announced Mr Perkins.

"And we've found out about Tom Troone!" Miss Muggins burst out triumphantly.

Harvey Angell gave them both his full beam. "First-rate detective work," he said. "I'll know who to call on when I'm stuck on a mystery Homing job."

"It was nothing," said Miss Skivvy, blushing. "We just made a few inquiries."

"But we learnt an awful lot," said Miss Muggins eagerly.

"Tell us!" said Harvey Angell, sitting cross-legged on the rug. They all joined him.

"Lottie was Tom Troone's sister," began Miss Skivvy.

"But she drowned, poor dear," continued Miss Muggins. "And it should have been him. Tom Troone."

"Yes," said Miss Skivvy, "she went out in his place, you see – though we didn't hear why – and she and her father both drowned."

"So *that's* why he thinks she hasn't forgiven him," said Henry.

"And why he hasn't forgiven himself," said Harvey Angell quietly.

"Poor old fellow," said Mr Perkins and Henry saw

him wipe his eyes with the back of his hand. "*He's* more haunted than the house."

"Perhaps," said Henry, "if I give Lottie her sea glass and tell her about her brother and how bad he feels, that will make everything all right."

"It's possible," said Harvey Angell, "but not if Tom Troone is still locked in sorrow. And there's something else you're forgetting . . ."

"What?" asked Henry.

"Time, for Lottie, isn't the same as time for you," said Harvey Angell. "A day for you might be a year for her . . . or a second . . ."

"But I've only got six days left," cried Henry. "Surely she knows that?"

"How can she?" Harvey Angell asked. "All she knows is that you've come to live in her house."

"You mean she doesn't know I'm only here on holiday," said Henry slowly.

"She might or she might not," said Harvey Angell. "We've no way of knowing."

"So what can we do?" asked Henry.

"Well," said Harvey Angell, "without Tom Troone's help we'll need all the Energy of the Connecting Kit to help us. I'll do my best for you, Henry."

"I wonder," said Miss Skivvy, "if anyone is feeling hungry?"

"A cup of tea might be rather welcome," said Mr Perkins.

"And perhaps scones?" suggested Miss Muggins.

"With strawberry jam?" added Miss Skivvy.

"And maybe a cake . . ." said Miss Muggins.

"Or lemon meringue pie," said Miss Skivvy.

They all made their way back to Sibbald House. Miss Skivvy flung open the kitchen door.

"A feast! An absolute feast!" cried Mr Perkins.

"No one would guess, Perkins, that you'd already eaten four ice creams, two fish and chip suppers and several very large doughnuts this week," said Aunt Agatha.

"I suppose you've been keeping a record," said Mr Perkins sitting down at the table.

"Of course," said Aunt Agatha. "I have to consider your well-being."

"And your purse," said Mr Perkins, helping himself to a scone.

"This amount of food should last us the rest of the week," said Aunt Agatha.

But it didn't of course. Everyone seemed astonishingly hungry – including Aunt Agatha.

Henry found a small box, set it in the middle of the table and put the sea glass on top of it. It glowed at him as he munched his way through scones and strawberry jam, lemon meringue pie and banoffie tart.

Surely, surely, when he put the sea glass in Lottie's room she would materialise for one last time?

* * *

But although he washed the sea glass and polished it so that it shone more richly than any emerald and then set it on Lottie's dressing table in the hidden room, there was no sound or sight of her that night.

Harvey Angell had plugged in the Connecting Kit. The Centuries Clock – carefully set at seven minutes past twenty – hummed quietly to itself as if it was brooding over all the years gone by.

"If I hear anything at all, I'll wake you, Henry," Harvey Angell promised.

"What if she comes very quietly, takes the sea glass and goes?" worried Henry. "And then I won't be able to say goodbye."

"It's a risk," said Harvey Angell, "but my guess is that she'll want to see you."

But the ninth, tenth and eleventh day of the holiday passed and the house – and Lottie – stayed silent. Each morning when he got up and each evening before he went to bed, Henry crawled through the hatch into the hidden room. Sometimes he felt as if he was crawling back not into Lottie's past, but his own. And sometimes the room seemed wholly empty, as if no one had ever lived there. And sometimes he had the notion that Lottie had been and gone and he'd only just missed her.

One morning he held the cool sea glass in his hand and spoke into the air. "I've found it, you know," he said. "Your Lucky. So I wish you'd come back. I mean, materialise. I haven't much time left . . ." It sounded silly, talking to himself like this. And Lottie – well, Lottie had all the time in the world. Or on the circuit.

The house itself seemed moody. Coming back after a day on the beach or walking the cliffs, either it felt quiet and undisturbed or there was a certain quiver in the air, an inexplicable warmth in the seat of a chair, a mug in the sink that surely hadn't been there before. Did Lottie walk about the house when they were all out? Was it easy to materialise when there was no one there to see you? Did she wander invisibly . . .?

The holiday days drifted by. The sun stayed out. Henry went swimming, ate enough ice cream to last a life time, walked up to the Harbour with Mr Perkins and watched the fishing boats going out. *Constant Hope II* was his favourite. It seemed to suggest he should keep on hoping.

By now Henry could hardly imagine going back to Ballantyre Road. It was as if he'd said goodbye to the Henry that had lived at 131, the Henry who was always awkward and embarrassed. Henry Oddity. A jumble-clothed, jumbled-up Henry. And become . . . Well, he didn't quite know. A *new* Henry.

"I think you've grown at least two inches on this holiday, Henry," said Mr Perkins. And Henry thought yes, inside and out.

Sometimes he and Harvey Angell walked to the end of the strand of rocks – the seagulls' 'platform' – and Harvey Angell played his flute and Henry closed his eyes and felt the sun very warm on his knees and eyelids. The seagulls swirled about Harvey Angell's head as if they preferred his tunes to their own calls.

When Henry looked back at the others on the beach – Mr Perkins building a sandcastle, Miss Skivvy swimming in her armbands – they all looked very small.

"Like children, aren't they?" said Harvey Angell. "I think there's a ghost of a child in everyone."

"Perhaps I've got the ghost of a grown-up," said Henry and for a moment felt sad.

But Harvey Angell slapped him on the back and gave him the full beam. "You've plenty of time for that," he said. "And I think I've got the answer."

"To what?" asked Henry. "Growing up?"

"No one's got the answer to that!" said Harvey

Angell. "No, I mean the answer to the problem of Lottie."

Then it was Henry's turn to beam. "What is it?" he asked urgently. "Tell me!"

"Seagulls," said Harvey Angell. And he stood up, spreading his arms to the sky as if he was going to fly off with them.

"Bu how can seagulls help?" asked Henry.
"There's an old legend," said Harvey Angell, "that when a fisherman dies he comes back as a seagull."

Henry looked again at the seagulls, screwing up his eyes and trying to turn them back into men. He remembered the photographs of fishermen he and Mr Perkins had once seen in the city museum, bearded men in round hats and wellingtons with nicknames like Nobby Clarke or Long-Legs Jones. Could that seagull perched at the end of the strand be Long-Legs returned?

"But even if the legend is true," said Henry, "how does it help us with Lottie?"

"I believe if we can persuade a few seagulls to come to the window of Lottie's room and if she hears their call – then that will bring her."

"And I suppose there's nothing easier!" said Henry. "You just click your fingers and command a few seagulls to appear on the window-sill at midnight!"

"There's no need to mock," said Harvey Angell. "As it happens it *is* very easy – but not at midnight."

"When, then?" asked Henry.

"Dawn tomorrow," said Harvey Angell promptly.

* * *

At first light Henry crept out of bed, slipped the sea glass in his pyjama pocket and knocked quietly on Harvey Angell's door.

"We won't wake the others," Harvey Angell had said. "Ghosts prefer to talk one-to-one and you're the one Lottie's chosen."

Harvey Angell was already up and dressed. He'd pushed up the hatch into the secret room. Through the gap Henry could see the red light of the Energy Charger and hear the ticking of the Centuries Clock.

"Watts and volts, watts and volts,
Better by far than thunderbolts,"

said Harvey Angell. "Morning, Henry. I think we have good vibes. Listen to the Clock."

Henry listened. He remembered how it had behaved in Ballantyre Road on the night when, finally, the secrets of the past had become known and sadness, like the end of winter, lifted. Now the Clock was doing the same thing – going faster and faster as if it planned on outwitting time itself. The red finger of the Energy Charger leapt to 'Full Power'. Henry felt his legs go so trembly that he had to sit down.

Harvey Angell, to Henry's surprise, had half a loaf of bread on the bed. He'd cut himself a slice and was eating it raw. "Breakfast!" he said. "Mine and the seagulls."

"Oh!" said Henry, feeling rather disappointed. "I thought you were going to work some magic."

"Sometimes," said Harvey Angell, "a little intelligence plus a dash of imagination works just as well as magic. I often think magic is a kind of combination of the two. Now . . . are you ready?"

Henry's throat was so tight he could only nod. One behind the other – Harvey Angell first – they crawled into the hidden room.

Despite the excitement of the Centuries Clock and the Energy Charger, the room had a still, pearly, expectant light. Harvey Angell inched up the window, broke off an edge of loaf and crumbled it on the sill.

"Perhaps a little music too," he said and taking the silver flute from the pocket of his dungarees, he began to play very softly. (So there is *some* magic, thought Henry.)

Within seconds – or so it seemed – a single seagull (Long-Legs Jones?) had landed on the window-sill. Harvey Angell didn't look round. He kept on playing and the gull, when it had finished eating, began answering the music with its own haunting, homesick cries.

The light in the room began to shimmer as though some electricity was in the air. Very faintly Henry heard a few squeaks, some muffled noises – rather like the noises Aunt Agatha made when she was changing the cover of the duvet and had got stuck inside it. Then there was a louder "Oh", a long "Owww", a last surprised "Ooooh!" and Lottie was there!

There, but somehow paler and less substantial than when he'd last seen her. It was as if night, and not this early morning light, was her natural element or that she was thinner on each return.

The Centuries Clock gave a last, furious 'ticktock-ticktockticktock' and fell silent. The gull gave a single screech, rose into the sky and headed seawards. Harvey Angell tucked his flute back in his pocket and quietly left the room.

And suddenly all Henry's worry, struggle and sleepless nights snapped into temper.

"I thought you were *never* coming back," he said. "And I've spent days searching for your Lucky – and here it is!"

He took the sea glass from his pyjama pocket and tossed it to her.

Lottie caught it and held it against her cheek as if her cheek was burning and only the sea glass could cool it. Instantly her eyes – eyes, Henry now saw, that matched the colour of the sea glass exactly – filled with tears. Henry's anger melted.

"Thank you," said Lottie. "And I'm sorry if I kept you waiting. You see time isn't the same for me as it is for you. I thought it was only yesterday that I saw you."

"Well, let's say a few yesterdays," said Henry. "And now will you tell me why the sea glass is so precious?"

"My mother gave it me," said Lottie. "She told me to keep it in my pocket and I'd always have my bearings."

"What did she mean?" asked Henry.

"Why, that I'd always have a piece of the sea in my pocket and so wherever I was I'd feel at home. My mother said that to feel at home in the world was to be happy. Lucky. So I've always thought of the sea glass as my Lucky. Only – " and Lottie's voice became sad, "that night I forgot to take it with me . . ."

"You mean the night you. . . ." Henry hesitated. Did ghosts remember dying?

"Yes, the night I drowned. Father and I and all the crew of *Constant Hope 1* – that was our boat, you see, and Father was the skipper. He never wanted to take me. Said a girl's place was in the home, or with the fisher-lassies on the quay. Said I was an oddity because I always wanted boy's work. And I did! I was so happy that night – until the storm came and swept us on to the rocks and ripped the bottom out of the boat and the sea took us . . . took us all."

"There's a *Constant Hope II* now," said Henry. "I've seen it in the harbour."

"So something of us has survived," said Lottie. "I'm glad."

There was a long silence between them. Then on an impulse Henry took the scarlet ribbon from his pocket and gave it to her.

"Why, it's my birthday ribbon," said Lottie, smiling. "My last birthday! Thank you!"

"I wanted you to have it," said Henry, "before I went home."

"Home?" said Lottie. "Isn't this your home? I thought you'd come to take over the house – it's been empty so long now."

"No," said Henry, "We're only here on holiday." And he told her about his home at 131 Ballantyre Road and the business of the city. "I wish you could come with me," he said.

Lottie smiled. "But I'm on my way, you see. And it's so much more comfortable without a body. What a very heavy thing a body is, don't you think?" And Lottie looked down at her own. It looked anything but heavy to Henry – almost as if she could be blown over. Anyway, he thought with a slight shiver, being without a body was not something he fancied.

"So we'll never meet again," he said sadly. "I'm going to miss you. And Sibbald House."

"Well don't," said Lottie firmly. She'd perched herself on the dressing-table stool and was twirling round on it. "Just because you won't see me, like your other friends – and there will *be* other friends, Henry – doesn't mean that I'm not one. We all have so little time, but you've shared some of my time and I've shared some of yours. And besides there's still the mending to do."

"Your voice is getting fainter," said Henry, suddenly frightened.

"I know," said Lottie. "I don't have long, I'm afraid."

And as she spoke Henry heard the seagull again. It had flown back to the window-sill and its call was urgent, as urgent as if it was calling Lottie away, away over the North Sea, away beyond Henry's imagination.

"Don't go yet!" he begged.

"I must . . . I must," said Lottie and then she did the last thing that Henry was expecting. She thrust the sea glass back into his hand.

"Thank you for finding it, Henry," she said. "Thank you for finding *me*! Give it to Baggsy for me . . . please . . . for the mending . . . Please. PLEASE."

She was fading from the feet up.

"Baggsy? Who's Baggsy?" cried Henry desperately. He felt like someone who'd climbed to the top of a mountain only to find there was another, higher one, behind it.

But it was too late. There was a shimmer in the air. The Clock began a slow and regular 'tick tock tick tock'. The gull was gone. And so was Lottie.

Henry stood holding the sea glass. For a moment he wanted to cry, but somehow the sea glass, as cool in his hand as it had been against Lizzie's cheek, steadied him. He wished he could keep it for ever and ever. Instead he'd have to find 'Baggsy'.

* * *

"It's very strange," said Aunt Agatha at breakfast, "but this morning the house feels quite different. Lighter. Happier, even."

"Yes," said Miss Muggins, "I woke early and there was such a warm contented feeling in my room that I fell asleep again. I dreamt I was a child looking for something I'd lost."

"Odd," said Miss Skivvy. "I dreamt I was ten again and back at school."

"Seagulls," said Mr Perkins. "I was trying to read a poem in the park and seagulls kept interrupting me. And then I thought I smelt herrings. Fancy a dream with smells in it! And then when I woke up I had that lovely feeling I used to get when I was a boy and there was a whole day of sunshine ahead of me."

Henry and Harvey Angell exchanged grins.

Aunt Agatha spotted it. "What's going on?" she asked. "I don't want any more secrets this holiday please, Henry."

"It's Lottie," said Henry.

"Ah!" said Aunt Agatha with a huge sigh of relief. "Has she appeared? Have you given her the sea glass?"

"Yes. And no," said Henry. "She came this morning . . ."

"For the last time," said Harvey Angell, buttering himself another large crust of bread.

"And I did give her the sea glass but she gave it me back. Told me to give it to someone called Baggsy – for the mending, she said. And then she vanished before I could find out who he – or she – was."

"It's Tom Troone!" shouted Miss Muggins and Miss Skivvy together. "Tom Troone is Baggsy!"

"That was his nickname because he always wore baggy trousers," said Miss Skivvy.

"Well, why on earth didn't you tell us before?" said Aunt Agatha crossly.

"It didn't seem important," said Miss Skivvy defensively.

"We might have forgotten," said Miss Muggins, "until now."

Henry took the sea glass from his pocket and polished it on his sleeve. "Tom Troone doesn't deserve it," he said sulkily.

"Deserving doesn't come into it," said Harvey Angell. "Your job, Henry, is to pass on the Energy. To mend the connections."

"All right," said Henry. "But I won't knock on his door again. I won't. I'll post it to him. With a letter."

For the first time ever, Henry saw Harvey Angell looking both sad and doubtful.

But I don't care, thought Henry. I just don't care!

CHAPTER 19

Dear Mr Troone (wrote Henry),

It wasn't very nice of you, renting a haunted house to people on holiday like us. And putting 'Child essential' in the newspaper like that and then never wanting to talk to me. It was all very scary at first and Miss Muggins and Miss Skivvy take fright easily and so does Mr Perkins because he's a poet and has trouble with his nerves.

So I don't know why you did it really, because I know Lottie was your sister and if she was *my* sister I'd have looked after her – well, even her ghost – better than you did. I expect you feel bad, her drowning like she did, but you didn't have to leave her lost in the house. Stuck in time, Harvey Angell says she was (I think you have met Harvey Angell, he was the man playing the flute). How would you like it? I mean being stuck in time?

Anyway, all Lottie wanted was her Lucky which I found (it was down the side of the sofa) and I had to search for days and you would have known what it was and could have found it easily. So here it is. Lottie wants you to have it. I don't think she will trouble you again.

Goodbye, Mr Troone,

Henry

PS But we have had a good holiday.

Henry folded up the letter. He found a box of paper hankies and wrapped the sea glass in it. Then he put it in an envelope with the letter, stomped up Cove Wynd for the last time and without even peeping through a window, pushed the package through Tom Troone's letter box.

He walked slowly back to Sibbald House. Up near the harbour he saw two fishing boats setting out. He heard their engines flare up and saw them judder into life. They tugged at his heart, going out to sea like that. The boat Lottie had gone out in would have been very different – no big crane and no engine – but it would have sailed from the same place and Lottie herself would often have walked this very road back to Sibbald House. Then one night, all of a sudden, unexpectedly, she'd been stopped. Stopped in time. But I'm not stopped, thought Henry, quickening his walk. I'm just beginning. And carrying on. Carrying on for me *and* Lottie.

* * *

Back at Sibbald House, Aunt Agatha and Mr Perkins were packing for home.

"You surely can't be taking that jar of marmalade," said Mr Perkins. "There's only a spoonful left in it."

"Waste not, want not, Perkins," said Aunt Agatha, rescuing the jar from the rubbish bucket.

Harvey Angell was packing too. Henry went and watched him unplugging the Energy Charger and disconnecting the Centuries Clock. He gave his flute a quick polish on the front of his dungarees and then slid it into his tool bag.

Henry looked about him at the hidden room, Lottie's room. All the drapes were back over the furniture – Aunt Agatha must have tidied up – but the empty room was full of sunshine.

"What the house needs now is a new family," said Harvey Angell. "And I expect it will find one soon."

Henry was just about to say that he thought it was people who found houses and not houses that found people when there was a knock at the door and then Aunt Agatha's voice calling up the stairs, "Someone to see you, Henry."

"Tom Troone, I expect," said Harvey Angell calmly. And so it was. But as the sunshine had got into Lottie's room, so the sunshine had got into Tom Troone's face. The many lines in his face that had all turned downwards now turned upwards and he was smiling. The smile carried on into his eyes – eyes the colour of the sea glass, eyes like Lottie's.

"I think I've some explaining to do," said Tom Troone as Henry and Harvey Angell came into the sitting room. Tom Troone sat on the mouldy sofa, his long legs in their sea boots stretched out before him and one great paw resting on the arm of the sofa. He looked very at home.

"I should just think you have," said Aunt Agatha before Henry could open his mouth.

"And Henry to thank," said Tom Troone, ignoring

Aunt Agatha. "You see, Henry, as I expect you know, this was our house – Lottie's and mine. Our dad was a skipper then. He had two boats and was doing very nicely thank you. Well enough for him to buy a big house like this and move us from the cottage we'd had. Our mam died young and so Lottie had all the household jobs to do. The cooking and cleaning and knitting and paying the crew and mending the nets. It was a hard life . . ."

"I should think living with you was hard enough," said Aunt Agatha, who was quite unaccustomed to being ignored.

Tom Troone kept his eyes fixed on Henry. "But our Lottie – well, we said she was a bit of an oddity – always wanting to go to sea. Used to beg our dad to take her. But he never would."

"I should think not," said Aunt Agatha.

"Being odd," said Henry, loudly and clearly, "often means being yourself. Which is the nicest thing of all to be."

"Why, you sound just like our Lottie!" said Tom Troone. "Well, as I was saying, there came a night when I had a date with a girl – prettiest little thing she was, Annie MacReadie's elder sister in fact – and me, well, I was quite besotted. So I slipped out of the house early, so Dad wouldn't find me. I'd given my mate, Fergus Dunbar, the tip-off. He was to take my place in the crew. He was to be on the quayside, waiting."

Tom Troone paused, took out a none-too-clean handkerchief and wiped his watery old eyes.

"I should have known better," he continued. "Fergus Dunbar! Forgetful Fergus, they called him. He was hard pressed to remember what day of the

131

week it was! So where was he that night when he should have taken my place? 'I'm sorry, Baggsy,' he says to me when it's all too late – too late for Lottie, too late for my dad – 'I forgot.' He forgot! Well, that was Lottie's chance, wasn't it? Her one and only chance to join the crew. And she took it. Oh aye, she took it!"

Tom Troone fell silent and they all waited.

"It was one of those freak storms no one expected," he said.

"So she never came back," said Harvey Angell.

"No," said Tom Troone, and his 'no' echoed and wavered round the sitting room. "No, neither she nor my dad ever came back. And afterwards . . . well, I couldn't stay here. Not with Lottie haunting the place like she did and me always taking the blame. I shut up the house and rented the cottage in Cove Wynd. I was going to sell this place, but no one would buy it, and I soon realised why . . ."

"Lottie wouldn't let them," said Harvey Angell.

"That's right," said Tom Troone. "Created havoc whenever anyone came to view. Moaning and crying and so on. Scared everyone off . . . It was as if she wouldn't let the house go. Or me . . ."

"But why didn't you talk to her yourself?" Henry burst out. "You could have set her free on the circuit."

"Hush, Henry," said Harvey Angell.

"I don't rightly know what you mean by the circuit," said Tom Troone, "but at first I was too frightened and too guilty to talk to her. Then when I tried, it was too late. She'd stayed the same age, you see, but of course I hadn't. It was as if she didn't know how to talk to me any more. That, or she still blamed me. She had every right to blame me. I've blamed myself for – well, for nearly seventy years. But now I know – now I've got the sea glass, I know. Lottie's forgiven me. This is her way of saying so." And Tom Troone held the sea glass against his cheek, much as Lottie had done.

"So you thought that maybe if a child the same age as Lottie came to stay . . ." Henry said slowly.

"Yes," said Tom Troone. "That it would break the haunting. Forgive me, but I'd carried the burden so long I just wanted her away. I'm not getting any younger you see and more and more it troubled me, thinking of Lottie's spirit shut up in here, trapped. So I took a chance and put that advert in the paper."

"I must have told you Henry's age when I replied," said Aunt Agatha.

"You did," said Tom Troone curtly. He turned to Henry again. "So I thought – maybe he's the one."

"And I was," said Henry.

"Which is why I think you should have this," said Tom Troone and he took the sea glass from his pocket and handed it to Henry. "It's done its work for me . . ."

"Yes," murmured Harvey Angell, "it's mended the connections."

"So I'll not be needing it," continued Tom Troone. "But you might. Lottie always said she felt at home when she had the sea glass in her pocket. And to feel at home in the world is a lucky feeling."

Tom Troone stood up and gave the sea glass to Henry. Henry couldn't stop himself from grinning ear to ear as the sea glass glowed in his hand.

For a moment, and for the last time, Tom Troone gripped Henry by the shoulders. Then the grip turned into a hug.

"Thank you!" said Henry. They were the only words he could find.

"Well," said Aunt Agatha, "I'm glad Henry is so pleased, Mr Troone, but I must say, taking into account all we've had to put up with here – a ghost, loss of sleep, searching for Lottie's Lucky – a little rebate on the rent would not come amiss."

But Tom Troone was looking his old fierce self again and every bit a match for Aunt Agatha. "You had the house for a song, woman," he said, "so no more of that. As for this fellow here – the flute player – he seems to get around a lot."

"That's true, sir," said Harvey Angell, giving Tom Troone his best beam, "I hardly know where I shall find myself next."

* * *

It was Harvey Angell who left first. They all gathered on the beach to wave him off.

"Will I see you again?" asked Henry.

Harvey Angell leant out of the cockpit. "Who knows?" he said. "But you know how to reach me, don't you?"

"But no, we don't," Henry called up as Harvey Angell switched on the engine and the rotor blades began to turn. "We just guessed . . ."

"It's a funny thing," Harvey Angell shouted back through the engine noise, "but I seem to have got warts on my fingers – as if someone charmed them there!"

Then the rotor blades were whirling and the engine grew louder and long after Harvey Angell was only a speck in the sky, they kept on waving.

When finally the sky was empty and silent, Henry looked down and saw the names Harvey Angell had written on the sand. They formed a complete circle like this:

Henry

Aunt Agatha   Mr Perkins

Miss Muggins   Miss Skivvy

Lottie

Henry found a stick and wrote 'Harvey Angell' in the middle. But it was odd, he thought, that the tide had been in twice and hadn't washed their names away.

"Angell magic," said Mr Perkins, answering Henry's unspoken thought.

"Time for us to go too," said Aunt Agatha. "I hope you know the way home, Perkins."

"I shall follow my heart," said Mr Perkins.

"And the map," said Aunt Agatha firmly.

Henry put the sea glass in his pocket. The sea in my pocket, he thought, and a whole world to see.

THE AWESOME BiRD

*D*ream bird - or real bird? Take off on a
fantastic flight of fantasy with the
magnificent, the gigantic, Awesome Bird.

'This is the first Really Unexpected Thing that's ever
happened to me,' said Laurie. 'You're more than Out-of-
the-Blue, you're the first proper adventure that's come
my way. Do we have far to go? Are we going to the Island?
Are we going There? And who is the Rabobab?'

The Bird didn't answer of course. Its wings had found
a smooth and regular rhythm that gradually soothed
Laurie into silence. He let his head sink into the soft
warm feathers of the Bird's neck and then he slept.

In his sleep he thought he heard the Bird singing and
the song somehow reminded him of Ginger's fiddle, only
it was a sweeter, slower tune and although it had no
words, Laurie new it was the Song of the Island.

THE AWESOME BIRD by Diana Hendry
RED FOX paperback, £3.50 ISBN 0 09 960521 X